D0951921

WILD
TURKEY

WILD
TURKEY
BY
ROGER L.
SIMON

A
STRAIGHT ARROW
THRILLER

By Roger L. Simon:
Heir
The Mama Tass Manifesto
Moses Wine Detective Novels:
The Big Fix, Wild Turkey

Library of Congree Catalog Card
Number: 74-18222
ISBN: 0-87932-082-6

Straight Arrow Books
625 Third Street
San Francisco, California 94107

Distributed by Simon and Schuster
Order number: 21975

Printed in the United States of America
10 9 8 7 6 5 4 3 2 1

For
Gloria Katz and Willard Huyck

1

The first time I saw Dr. Gunther Thomas — the renowned
Ph.D. in guerrilla journalism — was five AM on a Thursday
in December. I was tossing around all alone in bed when a
violent banging noise over my head woke me with a start.

"Wine! Moses Wine! Wake up, you bastard!"

I sat up and looked straight into one bloodshot eye next to
a black patch under a glistening, bald dome. Thomas wore
a silver-studded motorcycle jacket and was leaning through
my bedroom window, pointing directly at my forehead with
a leather riding crop.

"Wine, you creep! Think you're Philip Marlowe . . . I
know — a stoned Sam Spade. You're becoming a damn superstar, some kind of culture hero. *Newsweek, Esquire,* the
cover of *Rolling Stone.* Christ! In two months you'll be nude
in *Playgirl* . . . but you can't hype me. Wine! Let's get down
to it." The sweet smell of Wild Turkey blew over me from his
big, toothy grin. "Hey! Wake up!" he said, poking my nose
with his fancy stick.

I groaned and shook my head. Was this the famous writer
and culture hero or a lunatic escaped from Camarillo State
Hospital? Whoever he was, the noise had awakened my one-
and-a-half-year-old Simon, in the next room.

1

"Daaaah?" Simon said, more a question than a cry.

"Kids?" Thomas jerked up, cracking his head on the window. "Jesus, Wine, you must have a serious kink in your brain. We'd better start right now, the exclusive Gunther Thomas interview. Cut through the shuck. What do you do — speed, coke, yoga? I'll be back in twenty minutes with a photographer."

And with that he disappeared.

I stumbled into the kitchen, refilled Simon's bottle and dropped it off in his crib; then I sat down to wait in the living room for Gunther's return.

It was a long wait. About thirteen months. But when he did show up, at least it was at the more reasonable hour of eleven AM. I was standing at the sink doing the dishes, listening to Eddie Kendricks' *Boogie Down* and feeling sorry for myself, when Gunther came stomping through the living room in his Tony Lama boots.

"Here's the photographer I was telling you about. Anthony Streeter-Best." Gunther took off his white motorcycle helmet and waved it at a wasted-looking man in a torn fatigue jacket with three Leicas strapped around his neck. "Now let's get on with it. Moses Wine in action. A day in the life of today's private dick. Four or five pages in the *Stone* with pix."

Streeter-Best dropped to his knees and started snapping me from the side.

I poured another cap of detergent into the dishes. "You came at a bad time. I'm not doing anything now. My ex-wife's traveling and I've got the kids. No cases."

"Don't worry about it. We're more interested in your life style. Music, sex, cheap thrills . . . Besides, we already have a case lined up for you."

I turned off the water and dried my hands, heading for the record player. The back door slammed. Simon came waddling in with a guilty expression on his face.

"Potty," he said.

"Potty, my ass." I flipped him over on the linoleum floor

2

and pulled off his overalls. He was loaded. I glanced up at Gunther. "My biggest problem is a two-and-a-half-year-old who isn't toilet-trained."

"A very interesting case," continued Gunther. "A twenty-eight-year-old brunette stabbed in the back in her suite at the Beverly Wilshire, her naked corpse found draped across the chaise lounge, an upended bottle of Chateau Haut-Brion 1964 dripping plink-plink on the puce carpet."

I folded the diaper and pushed it away, groping for the pin on the counter with my other hand.

"And get this — the beautiful body turns out to be none other than Deborah Frank, princess daughter of movie mogul Maxie Frank and anchorwoman on the ABC morning news . . ."

"Shit," I said, puncturing my finger on the point.

". . . with a personal estate of three million and no will."

I grunted at him, sucking my finger.

"Ready to visit the scene of the crime?" asked the photographer. "Terrible stains . . . wonderful . . . terrible." He mumbled the words in a distinctly British accent, moving in for a tight shot, practically jabbing me in the eye with his lens.

"Don't mind Anthony," said Gunther. "He was hit in the neck by shrapnel in Cambodia and lost his sense of perspective . . . Well, how about it?"

I shook my head.

"What's the matter?"

"It's Saturday. I promised to take my son Jacob to the museum."

"What?" Dr. Thomas looked thunderstruck. "I haven't even told you who your client is."

I shrugged, snapping up the legs on Simon's overalls. I stood, went over to the back door and whistled for Jacob, who was shooting baskets with his friend Rolando. Gunther paced about the room behind me, stroking his helmet.

"You're making a mistake, Wine. You could use the exposure. All publicity is good publicity."

"Some other time."

"Our deadline is Wednesday."

"You should have thought of that a year ago."

"Sorry, pal. Nixon's kept me busy." He came right over against me, flashing a Mephistophelian grin and gripping both my shoulders like they were handlebars on his bike. "Think about it. The cover of *Rolling Stone.* 'Death and Vengeance: On the Case with Moses Wine' . . ."

I didn't reply.

"It's now or never, Wine. Play it safe or take it to the edge. Make up your mind."

He backed off, grinning to himself. I stared in his one good eye, thinking it over. Very tempting. Truth was, I was a sucker for celebrity. Maybe I even sought it out. And Gunther was good, especially his book on the Chicago Outlaws. What would he write about me?

But I shook my head. "That kind of exposure is lousy for detectives," I said. "It blows your cover."

Gunther looked at me in disgust. "Oh, sure. Can't handle it."

"Right."

"Got to take your kid to the museum."

"Right."

"Chickenshit . . . Come on, Tony." He nodded to his partner and the two of them started out, bumping into Jacob, who was coming in the back door bouncing his basketball.

"Guess what, Dad," Jacob said in his little grown-up voice.

"What?"

"I can't go to the museum."

"Why not?"

"Rolando's pop wants us to go fishing with him in Palos Verdes."

Gunther lit up like a pinball machine on twenty replays.

"Who are you?" asked Jacob, gazing up at the riding crop and the chrome buckles on Gunther's black leather jacket.

"Dr. Gunther Thomas. I'm here to make your father a legend in his own time."

"A what?"

4

"A star."

"You mean like Bruce Lee?"

"Something like that."

"Wow!" said Jacob. What did he know? Then he looked at me cautiously. "You don't mind if I go fishing, do you?"

"No. It's okay."

Rolando called him from the back yard. The kid let me have a quick karate chop in the ribs, picked up his basketball and ran out the door. "See you later, Dad," he said as the screen slammed behind him. I watched him cross the yard, straight and thin and getting so tall now.

"Maybe I'll reconsider."

"Reconsider?" Gunther turned around slowly and walked over to me. "Don't want to think I'm pressuring you, man."

Gunther moved from room to room, searching my house like a psychic panther, picking up vibrations off the walls and furniture. Every few seconds he called for a photograph of something he thought significant: my new blue blazer from Erich Ross, a Fred Astaire album, a tattered paperback — Balzac's *Lost Illusions* — on the bed table. He stopped at the picture of Alora Vazquez wedged into the corner of my bedroom mirror.

"Ah, yes, the beautiful chicana," he said, as if to himself.

We went out the side door to the driveway with Simon tagging along behind. The day was crisp and bright, good Los Angeles winter weather with good visibility. You could see all the way to the next ridge, where the eucalyptus trees ringed the rim of Elysian Park.

Gunther walked over to my car and ran his fingers along the top of the windshield.

"A '65 Jag XKE coupé. What happened to the Buick?"

"It got smashed up in the desert."

He opened the door and looked in. A naked GI Joe was lying in the back seat.

"Where's your former wife?"

"In Europe. Finding herself."

"Stuck you with the kids, huh?"

5

"No, actually, they're friends of mine. We like to hang out, prefer each other's company," I said, but he didn't look back, climbing into the front seat instead, resting his helmet on the dashboard.

"Let's take your car," he said. The Britisher got in the back.

"Where're we going?"

"To see your client . . . I've got the whole story set up for you, pal. Just stick with me."

A few minutes later we pulled up at the babysitter's behind the Logan Street School. I scooped Simon out of Gunther's lap and headed around the back of the stucco court, passing an alley where a couple of low-riders were tinkering with the rear end of a turquoise Impala. The yellow walls behind them were chipped and covered with fresh graffiti from El Ramiro and the Maravilla gang. I ran up the stairs to my left and rang the babysitter's bell twice. No one answered. The door was locked and the lights were out in the front room, so we went back to the car.

"We'll have to take Simon with us," I said, depositing the kid in the back seat next to Anthony. "Don't let him bounce around," I said and started down Echo Park Avenue, Gunther rolling a joint as I drove.

"You didn't ask me the name of your client," he said.

"Who is it?"

"Jock Hecht."

He passed me the joint. I took the mandatory toke and passed it back to Anthony.

"You're not impressed?"

"Sure. I saw him on the Carson show last week. He's doing a new book on sex."

"Right."

"What does he have to do with the murder of Deborah Frank?"

"The police think he did it."

"Did he?"

"Are you kidding? He won the National Book Award."

6

Gunther smiled mischievously. I shrugged and made a sharp turn on Sunset Boulevard, Anthony leaning over the front seat, shooting me with a snoot-nosed 135mm lens. I could see the caption in my mind's eye — *Tires SCREECH as dope-crazed gumshoe makes hard right on Sunset!*

2

Hecht was staying at the Chateau Marmont, an artsy residence hotel on the Strip, something like the old Chelsea Hotel in New York City. It catered to younger movie types and rock stars, capitalizing on its funky-chic appeal. From the outside it looked like a fading Moorish palace misplaced opposite a glass-walled bank and a couple of overpriced souvenir stands. Inside, an atmosphere of polite decay prevailed, the dark lobby and musty corridors providing perfect contact points for the high-priced dealers and other parasites who preyed on the guests.

We parked beneath the hotel and headed straight for Hecht's rooms, located in one of the more expensive bungalows out back. A number of people were having lunch by the pool, which had been drained for the winter. We crossed past them and walked along a row of cypress trees to Hecht's door. A flowering azalea in a Mexican pot stood at the front of the walk. Twenty feet away we started to hear strange noises coming from within, groaning and panting, and a loud, declarative voice speaking as if into a microphone:

"February 7 — The explorations continue. Freedom from hypocrisy and guilt. A return to the roots of civilization, the primitive races uncorrupted by the patriarchal morality of the West. The body and emotions no longer at war."

"*Keine krieg! Keine krieg!*" cried a woman in terrible German.

"Freedom from shame, freedom from possession," continued the voice. "Freedom in the pursuit of ecstasy. That is what we sought. The three of us — a dark, languid woman below me, a small-boned blonde above. We moved together like a three-backed serpent, undulating, vibrating. I was transcendent, unfettered, swimming like a Maori tribesman into the outstretched arms of our primal matriarchy."

More groans and screams of pleasure. The sound of furniture being kicked across the floor. Gunther started taking notes. Anthony shifted nervously from foot to foot. I looked down at Simon, who was staring at the bungalow in some confusion.

"Now, more!" shouted the voice. "Like Baudelaire said: 'The Queen of Spades, the dapper Jack of Hearts/ Speak darkly of dead loves, how they were lost.' Take me from the front and from behind and I'll take you again!"

"Aiiii!" shouted the women together.

Gunther banged on the door. "Open up in there, you heathen swine!"

"Who is it?"

"It's me, Jock. Gunther."

I heard some squeaks and the padding of bare feet on a tile floor.

"What do you want?"

"I've got the dick with me."

"I told you I didn't want to see him."

"It's Moses Wine."

"I know who he is and I still don't want to see him. I don't need a detective."

"We came all the way from East L.A."

"So what?"

"Let us in."

A weary sigh. "Oh, all right. Wait a minute."

I ran after Simon, who was heading off down the path

toward the pool. When I came back, the door was open. Hecht was standing there with a towel wrapped around his waist, a lavaliere mike dangling from his neck. In the doorway he appeared a stocky man, less powerful than he seemed on television and with more grey in his curly black hair. There were deep pouches under his eyes and the look of exhaustion about him. He must have been working pretty hard. The women were in the hallway at the rear, backing up against a closet. They wore bathrobes and were younger than I had expected. Both had beads of perspiration across their foreheads.

Hecht held the door open wider and Gunther, Simon, me and the *paparazzo* filed in. The bungalow was large and airy, furnished in thrift-shop eclectic, with filing cabinets and a couple of IBM supersonic typewriters stacked beneath a stairway to a second-story bedroom. A wide oak desk stood along the opposite wall with a bulletin board above it. A handful of broken amyl nitrate capsules were scattered on the floor beside a new Sony S124 tape recorder.

"So you're Moses Wine," said Hecht, taking my hand. "The hippie detective. You don't look as . . . outrageous as I expected." He looked up and down my white New Man slacks and blazer.

"Styles change," I said. "You've got to clean up your image. Besides, I was finding it difficult to investigate bank presidents in a tie-dye tee shirt and jeans."

"You still smoke dope, I hope."

"When I'm not on a diet."

Hecht smiled in agreement. "I switched to Wild Turkey myself . . . Well, good-bye. I'm sorry Gunther wasted your time."

"You're making an error, Jock," said Gunther. "You could use a detective. It'd be good publicity. An item in *PW*."

"I've had enough of that horseshit."

"I'm going to call Harriet. She'll tell you."

"Go ahead. Do what you want. Then leave me alone." He watched Gunther go off into the corner to make a phone call, then turned back to me. "I'm fifty years old and I've got too much more to do. There's no more time to waste on this Deborah Frank business." His voice trailed off as he glanced over at the young women. The blonde was still leaning against the closet while the dark one curled up next to Simon on the sofa. "These women have been good enough to take off from their sociology studies at UCLA to help me. We're investigating the theories of Bachofen and Otto Gross. We're going to prove that conventional marriage is a form of slavery conceived by men to upset the matriarchal order. It all goes back to the Judeo-Christian tradition. Monotheistic moralism robbed the world of pleasure . . . Have you read any of my books, Wine?"

"*Black Earth.*"

"Nothing since then?" He looked disappointed.

I shook my head. *Black Earth* was the World War II novel that made his reputation over twenty-five years ago. For the last decade he had been writing journalism.

"The one I'm working on — *Sex in America* — it could have been my best book."

"Could have been?"

"Will be . . . Who knows?"

From the corner we could hear Gunther's voice rising on the telephone. "Yeah, yeah, Harriet, I know. He *is* an egomaniac . . . above the law . . . yeah, yeah . . . I think so too." He cupped the phone and faced Hecht. "The New York *Post* just hit the streets with your picture on the front page. Big headline: 'Jock Hecht Under Suspicion of Murder.' Got out all the old dirt on your first wife. Random House is pissed and ready to cancel. Can you afford to give back $750,000, Jock?"

"Give me that!" Hecht grabbed the phone away and took it into the kitchen. Gunther grinned and went over to the bar, pouring himself a tall glass of Wild Turkey.

"Who's Harriet?" I asked.

"His editor. At Random."

He downed half the bourbon in one big gulp. I walked over to look at the bulletin board. The title of Hecht's new

11

book was printed across the top with a red marker pen —
SEX IN AMERICA: ONE MAN'S JOURNEY. The chapters were organized underneath on individual four-by-six cards with subjects ranging from group sex to open marriage. Some of the chapters were color-coded with little gold and silver stars; but it all appeared to have been hastily drawn, only a few details were sketched in beneath. A piece of scratch paper had been torn from a pad and tacked to the rim of the board — "Remember the preface to *Sons and Lovers*: 'For in the flesh of woman does God exact Himself.'"

"What do you think?" asked Anthony, coming up beside me.

"About what?"

"Will it be a bestseller?"

"I shouldn't doubt it."

Anthony nodded and started to photograph the bulletin board. "Stand there," he said, pushing me in front of it with Gunther, who was downing the Wild Turkey in glassy-eyed swallows.

"Best fucking bourbon in America," he said, while Anthony snapped the picture. "Reminds me of when I was covering the primary down south and went birdshooting with a couple of warped hillbillies from the Georgia swamps. Crazy bastards would stomp around with their transistor radios at peak volume, singing along and firing at random into the trees. 'Hey, Daniel Boone,' I asked one of them, 'you sure this is the best way to hunt? You'll scare the birds away before you even get a look at 'em.' 'Hell, yankee,' he answered, 'that don't make no difference. All's they got around here is wild turkey. And them suckers is so cautious the only way to catch one is shootin' blind at four hundred yards!'"

"Don't tell me about advances!" Hecht's voice came booming in from the kitchen. He was having a ferocious argument over the phone. "It all comes from the bank anyway!" He slammed down the receiver and stormed back into the living room, nearly stepping on my kid, who was on the floor in front of the brunette, playing with a string. Simon jumped up and ran over to me, clinging to my pants leg.

"They had some kind of damn meeting," said Hecht, shaking his head in disgust. "Random House and the heavies from RCA. They insist I hire a detective. They don't want me indicted for murder while I'm working on the book . . . Jesus Christ, the media is filled with paranoid nitwits!"

He slumped down in an easy chair opposite me.

"Why do the police think you killed Deborah Frank?"

"What do you care, gumshoe? They're gonna pay you five hundred a day. Take as long as you want. You'll get rich."

"I ought to know, if I'm going to work for you."

"If? . . ." He gave me a sardonic look. "I was supposed to be with her when she was killed. And we were known to be feuding."

"About what?"

"Oh, artistic rivalry . . . the war between men and women . . . the usual . . ." His voice trailed off. I stared at him impatiently, waiting for him to be more precise, but he didn't really seem interested.

"What kind of rivalry?" I asked again.

"She said I was a fraud, that I hadn't written anything decent since *Black Earth* and was exploiting the public. I went on 'Sixty Minutes' and called her a sexual reactionary. She did a show the next week, calling me an impotent drunk and a poseur. I attacked her in the *New York Review of Books*. She slashed back in *New York* magazine. I parried; she retorted, until . . ."

"Until you killed her."

"That's the theory."

"Is there any proof? . . . Witnesses?"

"None."

"It doesn't sound like much of a case."

"It's not."

"Then what's the problem with Random House?"

He sank deeper into the armchair, looking more like a middle-aged man whose life potentials were escaping him at an accelerating pace. His fingers brushed the carpet beneath him, sweeping the broken amyl capsules under the end table.

"The problem is my alibi." He spoke the words very softly.

"What's wrong with it?"

"You mean her. What's wrong with her?"

"All right. Her."

"She disappeared."

Gunther chuckled to himself, polishing off his Wild Turkey and firing up another joint without missing a beat. I looked back at Hecht. His eyes were half closed.

"Where were you when Deborah Frank was murdered?" I asked him.

"At the Kama Sutra Sexual Phrontistery on Santa Monica Boulevard . . . wrestling a live, nude girl."

I couldn't resist smiling.

"You think there's something wrong with that, Wine?"

"Don't be defensive."

"Well, I can do anything I want. I can go to an orgy with a dildo around my neck. I can fuck hermaphrodites and smell the toes of eighty-five-year-old ladies. I can blow every sailor from here to Tahiti if I feel like it. There are no laws to human nature. No laws except for those written by grey, officious men in the name of order — grey, officious men repressing our natural selves for their own power and violence. Our patriarchal rulers!" He stood by the chair and addressed the two young women, who were following Simon up the stairs to the balcony. "In the wilds, monogamy only occurs in the raven, the goose and the painted shrimp. The time has come to free ourselves!" he shouted. "Free ourselves!" Then he collapsed back into the chair.

I glanced up at Simon, who was perched at the top of the stairs jiggling a potted geranium. Despite Hecht's pronouncements, I noticed the author was quite content to let the women take care of him. But I let it pass. Simon liked the women.

"So you want me to find a live, nude girl?"

He nodded.

"What's her name?"

"Meiko."

"Meiko what?"

"I don't know. She was Japanese. She didn't speak English. And young — maybe seventeen, eighteen — like she just got off a boat someplace."

"Wasn't there anybody else in the, uh, Phrontistery?"

"The hostess — a woman named Rhonda. But she wasn't around when I came out and I didn't think to look for her until later. After all, I didn't have any idea Deborah Frank had been murdered. I don't usually need any alibis." He looked at me with curiosity, then threw his arms open wide and smiled disingenuously. "So, Moses Wine, what do you think? Do I look like the kind of man who would stab a woman to death because she called me a dirty name on the ABC morning news?"

"Seems unlikely . . ."

"Then you'll take the case . . . Clear my good name?" He laughed sarcastically.

"Take the case?" said Gunther. "He wouldn't miss it for the world. He'd blow a five-page spread I'm doing for *Rolling Stone* on how he saved Jock Hecht from a short trip to Death Row! Right, Moishe?"

I was about to make some clever retort when there was a loud crash and a scream from above. Simon had pitched the potted geranium over the balcony rail onto the tiled floor of the Marmont bungalow. Nobody moved to clean it up so I headed for the paper towels. Underprivileged fathers are used to cleaning up messes.

15

3

"How do you see it so far?"

"So far?"

"Yeah, you know . . ." Gunther leaned against the door of the Jaguar as I drove, switching on his own tape recorder, a pocket-sized, voice-activated Panasonic. "What would you say is exceptional about this case?"

"I wouldn't."

"What about Hecht? Not exactly the usual client, is he? A man of Faustian lusts . . . excessive . . . restless . . . endlessly searching . . ."

"You're the writer."

Gunther gave me an irritated look and reached for the bottle of Wild Turkey he had taken from the bungalow. He swilled it for a second, then passed it back to Anthony, who pushed his Leicas to the side and drank. "Where're we headed for now, mate? What's first on the agenda — the Kama Sutra Sexual Phrontistery?"

"To take care of Simon."

"The babysitter again?"

"No, my girlfriend."

"Ah, the Big Fix."

Gunther and Anthony exchanged knowing glances.

"Militant Mexican lady, isn't she?" said Gunther. "*Una revolucionaria* . . . You getting along all right?"

Anthony unscrewed a lens from one of his cameras and put in a 500mm. I winced and sped through the Macy Street tunnel into the barrio. Alora Vazquez, director of the Teatro Communal de Aztlán had been my girlfriend, off and on, for over a year. But lately things hadn't been going well between us and it was none of their business.

"I'd appreciate your staying in the car," I told them as I turned off Brooklyn onto Evergreen.

"Whatever you say, Thin Man." Gunther rewound his recorder and plugged in a fresh cassette.

I made another turn and pulled up in front of the body shop across from Alora's apartment. A couple of those stray dogs that infest the barrio nipped at my feet as I took Simon by the hand and crossed to her door, pressing the buzzer with trepidation.

She didn't answer right away. Through the window, I could see bags packed in the dining room, a canvas duffle belonging to the Teatro and a rucksack. A half gallon of Almaden Red sat on the table beside a large, unopened package of tostaditas. Alora herself was kneeling on the floor, stacking costumes in a cardboard box. When she came to the door and saw Simon, she didn't exactly look delighted.

"Can't today, Moses. We're leaving in the morning."

"The tour? . . . I thought that was next week."

"It's been moved up. We're going to Texas *and* New Mexico."

"When're you coming back?"

"Three months."

"Three months?"

She nodded.

"But I thought . . ." I studied her expression. It was hard and set. Devoid of compromise. I was upset. I still couldn't get used to the idea that a woman was free to go off and do what she wanted, when she wanted. As free as I was.

"You know your problem, Moses?" she said, reading my

mind. "You want a woman strong at the beginning, but more and more dependent on you as the relationship goes on. Like training a horse . . . Who are they?"

She pointed across the street at Gunther and Anthony, who had stationed themselves in front of the Jag. Anthony was crouching by the fender, firing his camera at us like John Wayne at the Alamo.

"Just some guys from *Rolling Stone*. They're doing this piece on the 'new detective.'"

"You're on your way to stardom, Moses. Mr. Flash." It was the first time she smiled.

I shrugged uncomfortably. Anthony stepped off the curb and switched cameras for a closer shot.

"Look, uh, can't I leave him here while you're packing? It's an emergency . . . kind of an important case . . . I'll be back by ten thirty."

"Ten thirty," she repeated noncommittally. She stared down at Simon, her arms crossed over her breasts where her nipples punched through a United Farmworkers tee shirt.

"Jock Hecht — You know, the writer. The police think he killed Deborah Frank, the anchorwoman for the ABC morning news."

"Oh."

I had a distinct premonition that this was the end, that when the Teatro Communal returned from its tour it would be all over for us. Asking her to watch Simon was only exacerbating matters.

I was about to tell her that when I saw Anthony edging across the street, circling in on us with his telephoto lens pointed at Alora's head. Gunther crept after him, clutching his tape recorder, a shotgun microphone extending down to the ground like a geiger counter. "Don't mind us," he said, drawing near. "Just go about what you were doing."

He raised the microphone and aimed it midway between me and Alora.

"Get away from here!" I said.

"All right. All right. Take it easy." He signaled Anthony

to retreat a few feet.

I turned back to Alora. She was running her hand through her hair, watching me. "It's okay," she said, taking Simon by the shoulder and drawing him to her. "You can leave him."

"Thanks . . . We can talk about it later."

"It won't work, Moses . . . Anyway, I'll be fast asleep at ten thirty. I have to get up and out by five in the morning." She touched my sleeve in farewell. "Good-bye," she said, a sense of ending about it. I didn't have the heart to tell her I meant when she got back from Texas.

Alora opened the door. I kissed Simon good-bye on his rosy cheek and they went inside. I stumbled back to the car, Gunther and Anthony trailing after me, recording our personal finale for posterity. I slumped behind the wheel. A sharp headache was coming on and I pressed my fingers to my eyelids, trying to avoid it.

"Now where?" said Gunther. "The Phrontistery?"

"Fuck you!" I said, leaning out and grabbing him by the flap of his motorcycle jacket. I should have slammed him in the jaw, but the whole embarrassing good-bye was bound to have happened sooner or later. I just made a note never to reveal anything too personal in front of Dr. Gunther Thomas.

"Yeah, the Phrontistery," I said, turning the ignition.

It was four thirty in the afternoon by the time we reached Santa Monica Boulevard in West Hollywood, the pseudo-sex capital of western America, and parked on a side street between *The Devil and Miss Jones* and some shocking pink storefront temporarily labeled "The Institute of Oral Love." I found the Kama Sutra Sexual Phrontistery just across the way, opposite a porno bookstore. A large Mediterranean type, dressed as a Sikh, guarded the front door beneath a Day-Glo version of Botticelli's Venus.

I walked straight past the place, glancing at the sign in the window ("Businessmen Welcome — All National Credit Cards"), and continued on to the next doorway, where I stopped to examine my reflection in the window. I started to

19

slick my hair down when Gunther followed me over.

"What're you doing?"

"Making myself straighter."

Gunther brightened. "Like Bogart in *The Big Sleep* before he goes into the rare-book store."

"Something like that."

He nodded and walked back in the direction of the Phrontistery. I pulled out an old glee club tie I keep with me for such occasions and had almost finished tying it when I started to get angry again. Reflected in the window, I could see Gunther and Anthony accosting the Phrontistery guard. Gunther took out his tape recorder to interview him. The guard backed away. Gunther complained. The guard looked annoyed. In a few seconds, an argument ensued and the guard looked furious. The big man began to make threatening moves at Gunther, his Sikh turban looming over the intrepid journalist. Anthony ducked behind them, taking quick shots of the action and not so furtive snaps through the window of the Phrontistery. Idiots!

I turned away quickly and headed off around the corner, putting as much sidewalk between me and them as humanly possible. After a few blocks, I stopped for breath in front of somebody's garage. Gunther came running up after me.

"What the hell do you think you were doing?" I said.

"Getting the full story, pal!"

"You realize you could have gotten us killed."

"I wanted to put you in jeopardy."

"That bastard had a gun under his cloak!"

"A Smith & Wesson .38 with a silencer." Gunther grinned at me.

"Congratulations. You win a merit badge in ballistics identification. See if it does you any good when he drags you out in the alley and sticks it up against your neck!"

Anthony came up behind us, looking out of breath and jowly. I stared back and forth at them, feeling more and more like a sucker. This superstar business was beginning to lose its appeal. It was making me unprofessional.

20

"Look," I said, "I've got a better idea."

"What's that?" Anthony was reloading color.

"I've got a contact who can get us to Meiko quicker than anybody."

"Who's that?"

I motioned them silently back to the car and looked inscrutable. We took the Hollywood Freeway downtown and then headed south on the Harbor Freeway. In a short while we were passing the L.A. ghetto. I turned off at the 89th Street off-ramp and made a left on Manchester past a liquor store and a Minnie Pearl's.

"Aren't we going a little far?" said Gunther.

"This man's the best," I said, slowing as we passed a black man in a green velvet caftan and mirror glasses leaning against a pawn shop. "Uga buga!" I shouted to him and stepped on it, whispering back to Gunther, "That's the signal."

Thirty seconds later we were speeding up 103rd past the Watts Happening Coffee Shop. We crossed the railroad tracks at the far end, turned sharply down an alley and pulled up in front of Simon Rodia's Watts Towers. Gunther and Anthony got out and stared up at the twin spires of broken pop bottles and beer cans jutting up into the twilight sky.

"You're putting me on."

I put a finger to my lips and led them around to the other side of the front gate.

"Wait here," I said and sat them down on a concrete slab advertising Clairmont Mortuaries. Then I walked back to the car and headed straight for the Harbor Freeway. Given the state of public transportation in L.A., I wouldn't have to deal with either of them for at least six hours.

4

It was pitch dark when I pulled up for the second time in front of the Phrontistery. I walked slowly to the entrance, giving the Sikh guard ample opportunity to associate me with Gunther and Anthony, but he only smiled at me and opened the door with a slight bow. Inside, I stayed by the entry a few seconds, adjusting my eyes to the dim blacklight and taking in the smell of cheap sandalwood from the incense burner. The walls were decorated with airline posters from South America. A chubby woman in satin hot pants and a halter top sat behind a desk eating a Bob's Big Boy. I figured her for Rhonda and guessed the place had once been a travel agency, probably quite recently.

"Howdy," I said. "My name's Harry from St. Louis. The company sent me out here for a week and my friend Phil recommended this place. You remember Phil?"

"Oh, sure." She looked up, disinterested.

"Phil said you were the best place on the street."

"He was right about that." She didn't sound convinced. "What can I do for you?"

"What've you got?"

"Massages — French, Greek or English . . . hot body shampoo . . ." She read from a bill of fare taped to the desk. ". . . Nude counseling . . . waterbed therapy . . . and the latest

22

thing, live nude wrestling."

"Sounds great."

"It's thirty-five dollars a half hour."

"Girl of your choice?"

"Why not?" But she sounded doubtful again. "Anything special you have in mind?"

"I go for Orientals."

She shook her head and shoved the last of the Big Boy in her wide mouth. "I think you've come to the wrong place."

"But Phil said you had a cute little number here . . . Japanese."

"Phil hasn't been around for a while."

"He was here last week."

"That's a long time in this racket, honey."

"Well, where'd she go?"

She stared at me, her hand picking involuntarily at a side order of fries. "You know there's something strange about you. You don't dress like a businessman from St. Louis."

"I'm in the record business." I reached for my wallet, displaying a stack of crisp bills. "Look, you gotta tell me where she is. Phil spent three hours getting me all worked up about her."

Rhonda shrugged, concentrating on the bills.

"You don't understand me. I've got a thing about Oriental women. I don't get off with any other kind."

I crouched over the desk, trying to look beady-eyed and perverted, but I could see Rhonda was used to it.

"Please, tell me where she is!"

I extended a twenty dollar bill. She sighed and waved it away, her fingers stained with relish.

"Save your money. I don't know . . . The boss is the only one who keeps the records in this place."

"Who's your boss?"

"I can't tell you that, honey. You want me to lose my job?"

"I've got to know!"

"Well, it's not the League! I'll tell you that. What's the matter with you, honey. You want to get yourself hurt? This

23

is Santa Monica Boulevard!"

"Look, the girl I'm after . . . I remember her name . . . It's Meiko!"

"Meiko!"

"Yeah. Where is she?"

"Meiko?" She repeated it again, breaking into hysterics. "Where'd you hear that?"

"Well, my . . ."

"Now I understand." She stared at me with a sly expression. "You're a friend of Jock Hecht! He calls all the girls Meiko!"

5

"Come on, Hecht! Open up, you sonofabitch!" I banged harder on the door of his bungalow. Inside, the lights were on and the television tuned to the Laker-Knick game, Chick Hearn blaring away. "Who are you trying to fool? Your alibi's worth shit!"

There was no answer.

I knocked again and peered in the kitchen window. A half-finished Chemex of coffee was on the counter next to a couple of croissants.

"Hecht!" I shouted. Still nothing. I grabbed hold of the door handle and twisted on it hard. But it opened easily. The door wasn't locked.

The living room was empty, as was the kitchen. I ran upstairs for a look at the bedroom. No one was around. Hecht's paisley-cushioned double bed was unoccupied. I ran downstairs again and checked the closets. Nothing. Then I stopped and stared at the Laker game. I remembered reading something somewhere that Hecht was a fan. At the moment, the score was twenty-one-all.

Then I heard a dripping sound mixing with the dribble of the basketball. Syncopating. I moved toward it. With a distinct premonition, I swung open the bathroom door. Hecht was in there all right, slumped backward over the toilet seat, blood oozing down the white porcelain from the gaping hole in the left side of his head. A Saturday-night special lay just beneath him on the grey tile floor.

I took a slow, deep breath from the diaphragm and stepped back into the living room. My temples burned. I clutched the arm of a chair, trying to center myself, trying to focus on the next necessary action.

When I was calmer, I looked around the room. There was no sign of a struggle. Everything seemed in place. A computerized digital clock read out the time to the second. It was 8:14:23 and moving fast.

Feeling more stable, I went and had another look at Hecht. His mouth was open slightly, the tongue depressed on his bottom teeth. His once piercing eyes had turned vague, almost fishlike. The gun was situated perfectly to have fallen straight from his right hand, which dangled motionless over the top of the toilet tank.

Starting to feel queasy again, I turned away. It was then I noticed the note in the typewriter. It was typed on Hecht's personal memo paper and wedged into the platen. I walked over to the desk and read it:

This is the last message from the desk of Jock Hecht. I have been unable to achieve my goals. The gap between my principles and actions has widened beyond any possible rectification. I am the murderer of Deborah Frank. I take full responsability for it. I exact my own retribution.

He had initialed the bottom of the page.

I read the note over again and then examined the top of the desk. It was neat and bare except for a roll of Ko-Rec-Type. The bulletin board appeared untouched, the cards as I had seen them. The metal files to the side were locked shut. I tried the desk drawers. The top one was filled with felt-tip pens and broken pencils, the second with stationery from hotels around the world. The bottom drawer was stuffed with newspaper clippings. A tear sheet from a magazine des-

26

cribed a marriage contract Hecht had made with his wife —
"The Death of an Old Institution Makes Way for a New
One." At the back was a black-and-white marbled notebook
like I used in elementary school. It was labeled "Journal,
No. 24" and dated from the end of January. There had only
been time for a few entries. I opened it and flipped through
to the last pages.

Sunday — Was Stirner correct? Is the ideal society a
union of egoists respecting each other's individuality?
. . . To reread: Franz Werfel and the memoirs of Alma
Mahler.

Tuesday — Don't forget clean shirts for book and author
luncheon at the Beverly Wilshire.

Friday — Cindy at Topanga, the first truly liberated
person . . . Send expense account vouchers to R. House.
And note to John Leonard about doing "Last Word" in
NYTBR on "Sex in Publishing."

I was about to copy out some names when there was a
knock at the door. I shut the book and closed the drawer.
Taking another fleeting glance at the corpse, I walked over
to the door and placed the chain over the latch, opening it
a crack.

"Who is it?"

A pale, redheaded woman about thirty was standing outside, carrying a small leather suitcase. Her eyes were unusu-
ally bright green and she wore a cable-knit sweater. No
make-up. She didn't need it.

"Who are *you*?" she asked.

"My name is Moses Wine. I'm a detective."

"A private eye?"

I nodded.

"Would you open the door?"

"Not until you tell me who you are."

"It's none of your business."

"I have to know."

"Have to know? I have more right to be here than you do."

"Why's that?"

"I'm Nancy Hecht. This is my husband's bungalow."

She held out the suitcase and moved closer to the door. I took off the chain and stepped hurriedly outside, shutting the door behind me before she could enter.

"I don't think you'd better go inside, Mrs. Hecht."

"Oh, Jock's up to something." She smiled sardonically. "Don't wory. I'm used to it."

She pushed past me and reached for the doorknob. I held her arm.

"You shouldn't go in!"

She stared at me for a moment, a look of apprehension crossing her face. "What's wrong?" she asked.

"Let's go over there," I said, pointing to a bench halfway to the pool.

"No, I'll stay here."

"I think you'd better sit."

"What's the matter? You think because I'm a woman I can't take bad news."

"I didn't say — "

"I'm going in, Mr. Wine."

She pushed forward with the suitcase again. She was right. If she had been a man, I would have told her straight away.

"Your husband committed suicide."

She let out a muffled cry and opened the door, running into the living room.

"Don't look in the bathroom!" I said, but it was too late.

She screamed, "Oh, my God!" staring at his body. She backed away in horror, groping for the couch. I shut the bathroom door, then stood there awhile, looking at her. She shook herself.

"When did it happen?" she asked.

"Sometime in the last hour, I would guess. After the basketball game started . . . The note's on the typewriter."

She glanced over at the desk, then back at me. "What were you doing here?"

28

"I was working for your husband, trying to clear him of the Frank murder. I came back to ask him something."

"How do I know you didn't kill him, that you didn't set this all up?"

"Would I have answered the door?"

She sat there a moment and brooded. "Did you call the police?"

I shook my head. "I'm going to do it now."

"I'll go upstairs and lie down."

"You want a drink?"

"That's all right," she said.

I watched her mount the steps, trying not to notice her ass at a time like this, then went over to the phone to call the police. After hanging up, I sat down on the couch and put my head in my hands. I was feeling pretty shaky myself. Outside, in one of the neighboring bungalows, somebody was having a party. I could hear the giddy chatter and the ploop-dee-ploop of a reggae band. The Caribbean wouldn't be a bad place to be.

The cops didn't take long to arrive.

And when they did, they were led by a familiar face.

"Well, well," said the stumpy sergeant, coming through the door like a second-hand Egyptian tank. "If it isn't the famous peacenik himself. And just when I thought short hair was coming back."

"You're looking kind of trendy yourself, Koontz. I notice you're getting into glitter." I pointed at the chrome-plated revolver strapped across his chest. "But save the Colgate Comedy Hour for after you take a peak in the bathroom."

He walked over to the door and looked in, followed by a couple of younger scrubs.

"So that's the great Jock Hecht. Wasn't there some other writer who did that to himself a few years ago?"

"Hemingway."

"Yeah, Hemingway . . . Where's the note?"

I motioned to the typewriter. He read it with painful slowness.

29

"Nasty people, these intellectuals. Hung up." He finished the note and started fishing through Hecht's drawer filled with clippings, pulling one out: " 'High Heels Anyone? Single, white male twenty-five interested in mild games wants to meet couples, transvestites . . .' Yucch!"

"Squeamish, officer?"

He looked up at Nancy Hecht standing on the balcony. "No, ma'am. I'm Detective Sergeant Koontz and these are Officers Higgins and Piccolo. We're very sorry about what happened here tonight. We were wondering if you might come down to the station to answer a few questions."

She nodded and started down the steps. Koontz ordered Piccolo to wait for the coroner and the rest of us headed out onto the so-called Marmont grounds. A crowd was gathering around the pool, drawn by the police car parked at the end of the bungalow. I heard someone whispering about a drug raid.

I walked right next to Nancy.

"I didn't mean to shield you. It was presumptuous."

"That's okay."

"My lady friend said I should have my consciousness raised."

She shrugged.

"I'll go down to the station with you."

"That won't be necessary."

We stopped at the police car. Koontz held the door open.

"Look, if you don't want to stay here tonight, you're perfectly welcome to . . ."

"I can handle this," she snapped.

She got into the car. I stood there, looking sheepish.

"You heard what the lady said, Wineradt," offered Koontz. "She doesn't need you!"

And he slammed the door and drove off.

6

It was still dark out when I was awakened by a jarring ring in my ear. I groped for the phone.

"Hello?"

"Hello, Mr. Wine. This is Harriet Whalen at Random House in New York."

"Uh . . ."

"Mr. Wine, are you there?"

"Yeah, I'm here."

"Because I'm sorry to say your contract with us is terminated. After the, uh, death of your client we feel it is no longer necessary to continue the investigation."

I didn't say anything.

"Mr. Wine?"

"You had to call me now?"

"What?"

"Do you know what time it is?"

"Er . . . here in New York it's almost nine."

"Yeah, well, er, here in Boss Angeles it's exactly twenty to six!"

I smashed down the receiver and buried my head under a pillow, trying to get back to sleep. But about ten seconds later Simon was jumping on my back with Jacob right behind him. The telephone woke them, too. This was going to be

31

one of those mornings when we ate our pancakes watching the sun come up.

Only that day there was no sun. It was overcast. The winds were from the north and clammy. By eight o'clock it was raining. I dropped Jacob at his school — where the kids seemed to spend more time weaving God's Eyes than learning to read — and drove on to Simon's babysitter, Nora. She was there this time, preparing for a psych exam.

I kissed Simon good-bye and went home feeling gloomy. A day ago, I had a high-paying case and prospects of my picture on the cover of *Rolling Stone*. Now all I could think of was Hecht's fishy mug on the toilet seat and Alora driving over the desert with a troupe of mustachioed Mexican actors, a soft down sleeping bag spread across the back of the van.

I put on a Billie Holiday album and slumped on the couch to watch the rain. It was coming down hard, pelting the window and blurring my view of the eucalyptus trees on the hill. A hunched figure in a yellow slicker was moving back and forth across the street, dodging the puddles. It was the mailman.

In a while, he headed in my direction, slipping a postcard through the slot along with some bills and then disappearing around the corner. I reached for the card. The photo on the front showed a rough-hewn peasant riding a donkey through a quaint Mediterranean village. The message on the back had been streaked from the rain. It was written to Jacob and Simon and came from Suzanne:

Hi Kids!
Am on the Island of Corfu at the villa of a wonderful French biologist. He thinks the salvation of man is through hydroponics. Ask your father what that means.
Love, Mom

I propped the card on the mantle and went into the kitchen to make some coffee, carrying a thermosful back to the living room and sitting down at the desk to confront my bills.

Inflation had struck with a vengeance. It seemed like my overhead had about doubled in the last month. I took out a marker pen and pulled out the bills, but there was a knock at the door before I had my checkbook out. I got up and opened the door. Nancy Hecht was standing there, her long red hair dripping wet.

"I didn't know it rained in Los Angeles," she said.

"How do you think we get mudslides?"

I opened the door wider. She entered, removing her damp cardigan and draping it over the arm of a chair. It was obvious she hadn't slept well in the bungalow at the Marmont. She was paler than the night before, dark rings under her green eyes. It gave her an ethereal, waiflike quality.

"I don't know where to start," she said.

"How about coffee?"

"Thanks."

I poured a cup while she looked around the room, focusing on the hash pipe from Afghanistan Suzanne had sent me as a birthday present.

"What did you think of Jock?" she asked.

"He was a little desperate, but so are a lot of people these days. I hardly got to know him."

"Do you think he killed himself?"

"I couldn't say. We read the same note."

She paused, as if she were thinking through its contents to herself. "He misspelled 'responsibility.' Can you believe that? A writer misspelling 'responsibility'?"

"I read somewhere Fitzgerald couldn't spell."

She sat and drank the coffee, her eyes beginning to mist over. "We have a daughter," she said.

"Where is she?"

"Back in New York. I called her this morning. I don't think it's hit her yet."

"Maybe you should go back."

"Not until I find out who killed Jock. He couldn't commit suicide. He was too . . . egotistical."

She crossed her legs and pulled her skirt under her. Out-

33

side I could hear sheets of rain pelting down on the corrugated roof of the garage, a dull clap of thunder far off in the distance.

"Did you tell the police?"

"Yes, but I could see they didn't believe me. They couldn't understand our relationship."

I gave her a questioning look.

"Open marriage . . . They thought that meant I was a whore. One of them tried to pick me up . . . Do you have a cigarette?"

"I don't smoke."

"Neither do I. I just thought . . ." Her lip started quivering. She was feeling what she had held in at the hotel.

"How about some cognac?"

She nodded and I went into the kitchen for the bottle.

"I can pay you," she called out. "Jock spent all his money. He said if he got too secure, he'd stop writing. But I have my own. I teach English at Hunter College."

I came back with a highball glass and filled it halfway up with cognac.

"How much do you charge?"

"A hundred a day plus expenses." More, actually.

"All right," she said, taking the glass from me and drinking it down quickly. From the look in her eye, she wasn't used to alcohol. She probably wasn't used to dope either.

When she felt better, she told me about her marriage. She met Hecht eight years ago when he came to lecture on his books at Hunter. She was a teaching assistant then, grading a seminar on modern American writers. Hecht was coming down off a disastrous marriage to a singer named Dolores Lee and was looking for someone more companionable, more his intellectual peer. He invited Nancy for drinks, then for dinner, then to a chic literary soirée in Brooklyn Heights. Soon they were going together. She moved her things into his plush brownstone on East 73rd. He introduced her as his main woman to important people in the arts and the media. When he asked her to marry him, she couldn't say no. He was Jock Hecht, after all; she a wide-eyed Ph.D. candidate writing her thesis on Emily Brontë.

"When did you decide to open your marriage?" I asked.

"We put a name to it three years ago. But we really practiced it from the beginning. Neither of us believed in monogamous relationships. They appear in nature only in the — "

"Raven, goose and painted shrimp."

She laughed. "Jock must have told you that! . . . Actually, he forgot the gibbon."

"Has it worked?"

She stopped laughing and looked at me. "I'd be lying if I said it hasn't been hard sometimes. All radical changes are hard. But people have been making unfair demands on each other for most of history. It's about time we tried to reform."

I poured her the rest of the cognac and she finished it off in one swallow. It wasn't even noon yet, but I was getting in the mood. I reached into the drawer and stoked up a carbonated water pipe, taking a couple of hits.

"Do you usually work stoned?" she asked.

"You need a little anesthesia in my line of work." She sank deeper into the couch. Her pale, white cheeks had flushed a bright red, matching the color of her hair. "Who do you think killed him?" I asked.

"It could be a lot of people. Jock made enemies easily."

"Anyone special you can think of?"

She nodded quickly. "Meyer Greenglass."

"The gangster?"

"Jock lived with him for a while to do a book on the Jewish mafia."

"What happened?"

"Jock never wrote the book. A week after he left, Greenglass got indicted on credit card fraud. The judge gave him two to ten years. They say he blames Jock."

"Where is he?"

"Terminal Island Prison."

"Let's go see him."

She looked at me to be sure I was serious.

35

I walked over to the closet, took out my raincoat and handed her a yellow serape with black fringe. "You can use this for now."

"Whose is it?"

"An old girlfriend of mine. It's not raining where she is."

7

"Meyer Greenglass is a distinguished gentleman and a model prisoner. Why do you want to see him?"

"I'm a private detective investigating the death of this woman's husband, a writer by the name of Jock Hecht. Hecht was a friend of Greenglass. We just need some personal advice, sir, nothing inflammatory."

The associate warden examined my license thoroughly and returned it to me. If he had heard of Hecht, he didn't show it.

"You understand Mr. Greenglass does not have to talk with you unless he wants to."

"We understand."

He stood and walked out of the office. I looked through the window at Terminal Island. Its crooked, palm-lined streets and sleazy maritime bars always reminded me of the capital of a dying banana republic. There was even a Veterans Administration building on a hill that looked like the Palacio Nacional waiting for a coup. That afternoon, the rain made it seem even more that way. The view of the modern port — the grids and shipping modules — was obscured in grey, leaving only the grimy, pastel row houses, the rusted hulls of dry-docked freighters.

In a few minutes the guard appeared at the door. He led us down a series of corridors, past open toilets and vacant cells, to an iron scaffold stairwell that led up to the Education Building.

"In there," he said, pointing to the door of what passed for a prison library. "He's giving you five minutes."

I opened the door to find Greenglass seated behind a plain wooden table under an arc light. There were books piled on the table and waist high around him. He was a frail figure with blotched, olive skin and gnarled, skeletal arms. A network of blue veins criss-crossed the temples of his bald head between wispy strands of thin, white hair. This was the stocky tough guy in the five-hundred-dollar suits who graced the *Daily News* Sunday supplement when I was a kid.

"Hecht's dead!" he said, not waiting for an introduction. *"Gay gesunt!"* He spoke in Yiddish like my great Uncle Benny, the Litvak. Good riddance, he had said.

"Why's that?"

"Why? You ask me why? After what I did for him?" Greenglass laughed and gazed rhetorically about the room, searching among the tattered copies of *Field & Stream* for some mysterious listener to corroborate him. "I take him into my house. I introduce him to my friends. I fly him to Bermuda, Palm Springs. I get him anything he wants. What does he do? Does he write the book? Does he do what he says? . . . And why not?" He raised his spindly arms in the air. "Women . . . women . . . all he wants to do is fuck!"

"This is his wife, Meyer. She just got in last night."

"Well, I hope he left you some money."

Greenglass stared at her, like the devil in the mirror staring at the naked lady. He sat up straighter with a strange glimmer in his eyes, smoothing down his few remaining hairs.

"He wouldn't even listen to my stories," said Greenglass. He pulled me over and whispered in my ear. I shook my head.

Nancy looked puzzled.

"He wants to know if you're Jewish," I explained. "He thinks you're good-looking but he wouldn't go out with a *shikse.*"

38

"Very funny," she said.

Meyer beamed and clapped his hands together. "What do you want from me?" he asked. "There's only four minutes left."

"What did you have against Hecht, Meyer?"

"I told you. He was a voyeur. He didn't deliver. No book."

"We heard that you blamed him for the credit card indictment."

"He had nothing to do with that."

"That's what it said in the papers," Nancy said.

Meyer looked up at her. "That was a story my attorneys put out to confuse the prosecution."

"It didn't help," I said.

"Why are you making such a *tsimmis*? Hecht is dead. He committed suicide."

"And you believe that?"

"Why not?" His voice turned momentarily somber, almost menacing. "Murder a fine girl like Deborah Frank. I'd kill myself too, I did something like that."

"You're certain he did it?"

"You find me somebody else."

Behind us, the guard was pacing back and forth, checking his watch. In prison, you had all the time in the world, except when you needed it.

"What about Hecht's friends? Did any of them come around your house?"

"I don't know his friends."

"What about phone calls? Was anybody trying to reach him?"

"Who should be trying to reach him? A pimp? The manager of a nudist colony?" He looked at Nancy again. "Why do you want to know if your husband was killed? What good would it do you? It's a blessing to be rid of him." He took a couple of expensive cigars from his pocket and offered me one. I shook my head. "Outside, you couldn't get better," he said.

"Three minutes," said the guard.

"Real Upmann's from Havana. I get them sent in from Switzerland without the wrapper." He took out a clipper and carefully sliced off the end. "Something else, smart young people?"

"Yeah. How come you let Hecht into your life? Isn't it a bit risky, having a writer nose about in your affairs, living like one of your family?"

"At my age?"

"Couldn't he stumble on something you wouldn't like him to see?"

Greenglass leaned back, striking a match and twisting the cigar slowly to get a perfect light. He puffed on it several times before speaking again. "That reminds me of a story . . ."

"Two minutes," said the guard.

"We were opening the Flamingo in Vegas . . . in '46, '47, around there . . . Did I ever tell you this one?"

"No, Meyer."

"No, of course not. I've never met you before, have I? A nice, Jewish *boychik* . . . Well, where was I? . . . In Vegas, '46, '47 . . . back at the Flamingo . . ." He stopped and looked around the room, puffing some more on his cigar. I had a strong suspicion he was trying to kill time.

"Get to the point, Meyer."

"Take your time, *menschele* . . . Well, back in Vegas, '46, '47 . . . a reporter flew in from California to interview me. Meyer, he asked, is it true you paid off the Governor of Nevada to get a gambling license on this hotel? Son, I said, not only did I pay off the Governor, I paid off the Secretary of State, three congressmen and a senator."

"One minute," said the guard, moving toward our table.

"I went to Washington and spoke with everybody I knew in the Department of the Treasury and the Internal Revenue Service, starting with the Cabinet and going all the way down to the humblest errand boy. I contacted all the key figures on the national news magazines. They were still publishing *Collier's* at that time and the *Saturday Evening Post*. Then I paid a call on the mayor of New York in Gracie

40

Mansion. And you know what?"

"What?"

The guard arrived at our table and stood between us. He held up five fingers.

"This man is trying to tell us something," said Greenglass.

"Just a couple of more minutes," I said.

Greenglass shook his head.

"You didn't finish the story."

"I have a class." He motioned to a glass-cased room off to one side with bar graphs on the wall. "I teach some of my friends here the rudiments of investment banking . . ." He stood and extended his hand. "Come again if you have any questions. And don't forget to bring the *madel*." He pinched Nancy on the cheek. "I heard so much about you and your daughter from your late husband."

Greenglass turned and, on the way out, joined several prisoners carrying notebooks. They entered the classroom, shutting the door behind them.

"Any other suggestions?" I asked Nancy.

"He knows how to avoid answers, doesn't he?"

"He's had practice."

We followed the guard, crossing the scaffold and heading back down the long corridors. He stayed with us until we had left the building and were crossing through the rain to my car.

I ran ahead of her and unlocked the doors before getting into the driver's side.

"What about Cindy in Topanga?" I asked her as we drove back across the bridge to San Pedro. "Does that name mean anything to you?"

"Is it supposed to?"

"The first truly liberated person."

Nancy smiled. "She must be a friend of Jock's."

"I found her name in his journal."

"What did it say about her?"

"Nothing. Except that she was . . ."

"Liberated?"

41

"Yeah."

"Do you think it's possible?" she asked.

"Being truly liberated?"

"Uh huh."

"I don't know. I still have trouble deciding who gets off the elevator first — me or a woman."

Nancy laughed. I looked over at her. She was leaning against the car window, pulling the serape about her. Her flaming red hair was bunched up on the glass, a swirl of color against the water drops.

"You know, you're the kind of woman who would make it all irrelevant."

"What?"

"Open marriage . . . freedom to fuck."

"Is that supposed to be a compliment?"

Suzanne and Alora were right. I had a long way to go, baby.

8

It wasn't as big as Hearst or Solzhenitsyn, but the suicide of
Jock Hecht had turned into something of a minor media event
by the time I dropped Nancy back at the Chateau Marmont.
It was just about noon. She wanted to call her daughter in
New York who was just getting home from school, but a
crowd of reporters ran up and started pushing little tape re-
corders through the window before she could get out.

"Mrs. Hecht, why did your husband commit suicide?"

"Mrs. Hecht, are there any posthumous manuscripts?"

"What do you think of your husband's sex life, Nancy?"

I backed up and pulled around the rear entrance of the
bungalow. Nancy and I got out and walked together to her
back door. We looked at each other a moment before she went
inside. "I'll let you know what I find out." She opened the
door and stepped in. "Lock it," I told her and waited until
I heard the sound of the catch before I headed off. I wanted
to talk to Cindy from Topanga, "the first truly liberated person," before the cops started to make a thorough study of
Jock Hecht's journals.

By two o'clock I was turning off the Ventura Freeway onto
Topanga Canyon Boulevard, climbing past the upper-mid-
dle-class tracts to the studied funkiness of the canyon. Vis-

iting Topanga was like examining an archeological dig, a layered cross section of the last twenty years — farmers and old-time radicals, under rednecks and chicanos, under hippies, rock stars and professors from UCLA.

Topanga Center was the meeting place for the hipper sectors of the community. It was the only shopping center south of Berkeley where seven-grain wheat loaves outnumbered Wonder Bread by five to one. But the whole place had a shopworn quality to it, a style frozen in time while the rest of the world moved on. In their tie-dye shirts and beaded headbands, the patrons reminded me of those Japanese soldiers hidden out in Pacific jungles for thirty years who didn't realize the war was over.

I walked around the side to an old post office that has been converted into a coffee shop. Inside, a few of the local denizens were sitting around drinking beer, running their hands through their greying beards and long, thinning hair. I sat down and ordered a cup of coffee, listening to the Bach cantata from the jukebox and searching the eyes of the four men at the table across from me.

"Any of you guys know Cindy?" I asked.

They looked up, surprised they were being spoken to. I repeated the question.

"Which Cindy?" said one of them in a stocking cap pulled low over his forehead. "I knew a Cindy back in Cambridge in '60 . . . waitress at the Golden Vanity. And then there was the Cindy on MacDougal Street who worked at the Folklore Center. And the Cindy at Bennington. And the Cindy who ran a bar in Torremolinos, the Cindy in France, the Cindy in Morocco. And the Cindy I met hitchhiking in Big Sur . . ."

"I mean a Cindy here in the canyon."

"Oh, that Cindy!" He laughed and shook his head. "Never heard of her."

The others stared at me blankly.

"She has something to do with sex."

"They all have something to do with sex, man . . . They're chicks!"

44

His use of the word jarred me. As if I didn't hear it every day.

"You mean Dr. Cynthia Hardwick."

I turned to a small, nattily-dressed man in the corner who was drinking espresso and reading a copy of *Le Figaro*.

"Do I?"

"I'm reasonably certain. Everyone calls her Cindy and she's the most important person in the sex business hereabouts. I've been her patient myself. She lives in the yellow A-frame, a mile up Fernwood on the right." He folded the paper in front of him. "Be sure you knock."

I drove out of the shopping center and up Fernwood into the posher section of Topanga — *the* neighborhood for lawyers, professors and screenwriters. Most of them drove Volvos and Peugeots and had clever little pseudo-Picasso sculptures in their front yards.

Cynthia Hardwick's A-frame was high on a cliff overlooking the entire canyon. I pulled up behind a new BMW with Arizona plates and got out in the rain to ring the big bell. Her house was finished in a kind of rustic kitsch with a hand-hewn redwood door, a copper buzzer and the name DR. C. HARDWICK surrounded in macramé. From inside, I could hear Deodato's "2001" blasting out at peak decibel.

It took a long time for someone to answer. Finally the door slowly opened on a small, well-preserved woman about fifty. She was wearing a bikini and wiping perspiration from her brow with a thick, blue towel.

"If you're here for the Growth Group for Unattached Men, it's been changed to Tuesdays."

"Dr. Hardwick, my name is Moses Wine . . ."

She looked me up and down. "Did you bring your signed statement?"

"What?"

"Your signed statement from a licensed physician or psychotherapist?"

I looked baffled. She took my hand and held it. "Don't worry," she said, "I'm not aggressive," and turned back into

45

the house.

I stepped inside. She climbed a spiral staircase to a loft, calling ahead of her. "Tony . . . Tony, you only have five more minutes. Why don't you come early tomorrow?"

Tony, a young blond man in a turtleneck, emerged at the top of the stairs, looking morose. She kissed him with fervor. "It'll work out," she said. "Remember. Patience, not performance, that's the key." He headed down the stairs, muttering to himself.

She beckoned me with her finger. "Poor Tony. His doctor sent him all the way from Phoenix and he expects miracles."

I watched Tony drive off in the BMW as I mounted the stairs to the loft. It was simply furnished with a couch, a couple of hassocks and a double bed. Cynthia sat down and looked me up and down like a friendly hunk of meat.

"The first thing we try to do is get used to being naked."

"Is that hard?"

"You find that easy, do you?"

"I used to go skinny-dipping in summer camp."

"Good. Let's get undressed."

She stood and took off her top. I started to unbutton my shirt.

"I hope you realize this could take a long time," she continued. "We have to relax and we have to be patient. That's the key."

She pulled off her bottoms and stood naked in front of me, her body in fine condition for a woman her age. I unhooked my belt and slipped out of my pants.

"Now, lie on your belly," she said. "We begin with sensitivity training, avoiding the erogenous zones. This could go on for days. As long as it takes."

I lay down on the bed, my face on a lime green pillow.

"There's something I haven't told you," I said.

"No, no. Don't be afraid. You're doing fine."

She leaned over me and began to massage my back, moving her fingers along the spinal column from the base of my neck down. I peered across the room as she worked.

46

There were some Guatemalan hangings on the wall and a flyer pasted on masonite — "Discover yourself! A week in Tahiti with Dr. Cynthia Hardwick, noted sexual surrogate."

"I hope you'll remember your physician's statement next time."

I tried to say something, but she cupped her hand across my ass and started stroking it from the bottom up. It felt terrific. "This is Masters and Johnson exercise number six . . . We could try stuffing by early next week."

"Stuffing?"

"Penetration with a limp penis . . . What form of dysfunction did you say you were suffering? Primary or secondary?"

"Dysfunction? I'm not here for dysfunction."

"What!"

"That's what I've been trying to tell you."

Dr. Hardwick backed off. I sat up on the bed feeling sheepish, a pretty stiff dick standing up at a forty-five-degree angle.

"I guess you're not," she said as I reached for my pants. "But there's no need to waste it!"

She smiled and started heading back toward the bed when we both were startled by what sounded like a volley of gunshots. Naked, I jumped up and ran to the window. Gunther was sitting on his motorcycle beneath the garage across the street, firing a .38 Magnum into the side of an abandoned truck. I threw open the window and leaned out to wave.

"Well, well. If it isn't Dick Tracy of the streakers!"

"What the hell are you doing?"

"Following you out from the Marmont, shamus." He took aim at the headlights and fired, smashing the glass. "You should keep a sharper eye on your rear-view mirror."

"Listen, who are you guys, anyway?" asked Cindy, slipping on a robe and coming up behind me. "I don't want to call security at the Institute."

"Don't worry. He's with me. I'm investigating the Hecht suicide."

"Suicide, my ass!" shouted Gunther from the middle of the street. "That bastard wouldn't off himself with such a cheap shot. We've got to get to the bottom of this. There's dirty work afoot here, Moses."

9

"So you're the renowned Dr. Gunther Thomas," said Cindy. The three of us sat around her coffee table downstairs, a full-sized portrait of Isadora Duncan looming above us. "I read that book of yours, *Dread in Tulsa,* the one about the oilmen's convention. Is it true all those crane operators shoot speed?"

"That or methadone."

"No wonder we have an energy crisis." She looked at Gunther in a manner calculated to tear the patches off his leather jacket.

"We came here to talk about Hecht, Dr. Hardwick," I reminded her.

"Yes, I know. Poor Jock. He tried so hard."

"Tried what?"

"What do you think? To free himself from the conventional mores of our society. That's why he spent so much time at the Institute."

"The Institute?"

"You know, the Liberation Institute. Surely you've heard of it. I'm one of the directors."

I shook my head.

"It's right around the corner from here. Just over Tuna Canyon."

"What happens there?" I asked.

"People come for a week or ten days. They leave behind civilization and its discontents to rediscover their natural selves."

"How's that done?"

"Oh, classes, exercises, study. Jock liked the facilities . . . the group baths and saunas . . . It's quite well endowed. It's a wholly owned subsidiary of the Sexual Liberation League."

Gunther stood and took out a box of ammo from under his jacket. "Let's have a look at this Institute." He headed for the door.

"Wait a second, Gunther." He stopped and I turned to Cindy. "The Sexual Liberation League. What's that?"

"A California holding company interested in human potential and leisure-time activities."

"What kinds of activities?"

"Creative. Loving. Experimental. You know . . . externalized."

"Can you be more specific?"

"Books . . . movies . . . import-export."

"Import-export of what?"

"Sexual apparatus from Hong Kong."

"What about massage parlors?"

"I wouldn't know." She started to look uncomfortable. "I really don't pay much attention, except where the Institute is concerned."

"And where *is* the Institute concerned?"

"Only on the funding level." She stood and started upstairs to the loft.

"Sounds fishy to me," Gunther growled. "Who's really behind this, Newport Beach?"

"I couldn't say . . . Possibly somebody at the Institute might talk to you . . . Possibly not . . . And now you must excuse me; the Sensory Awareness Seminar meets here in ten minutes."

She disappeared upstairs without waiting to be excused.

I left my card on her table and we went outside. "I'll give

you eight to three this league is just a cover for the CIA," Gunther said as we got into my car. "We'll leave my bike here. Head for Tuna Canyon."

I shrugged and drove off, climbing higher on Fernwood to the top, where it met Tuna Canyon Road. At the intersection a sign reading "Liberation Institute, 3 mi." pointed down a narrow, dirt road I had never noticed before. I turned and followed the fresh ruts along a dry river bed which was filling up in the rain, a tiny stream winding between the live oaks. We rounded a blind curve.

"You were pretty clever, trailing me out from the Marmont," I said.

Gunther smiled pridefully. "I'm surprised you were so easy to sucker."

"Nobody's perfect. We're being followed right now."

"What?" He whipped around and stuck his head out the window, looking back. There was nothing in sight.

"A '74 Lincoln Continental, powder blue with mag wheels, California license plate 328 KLR."

"You're putting me on."

I slowed by an old ranch house with a broken corral. Out front, a yellow mailbox had its flag up, a soggy newspaper hanging out the end. A couple of pintos were nibbling from a bucket of feed in the stable, their tails swishing back and forth.

I looked in the rear-view mirror and counted to ten. By the time I reached eight, I could see the Lincoln's wide grill rounding the curve on the cliff.

"You're not putting me on!" said Gunther. He reached for his gun.

I leaned over and grabbed his wrist. "You want to get us killed?"

He lowered his arm for the moment and I continued down the road. I didn't like our position, but for the time there was no alternative. The car behind us was following slowly, confidently. In another two hundred yards, I understood why. A green Ford van was pulled straight across the road

51

in front of us between the cliff and a sheer drop of a hundred feet. Two men were standing at the front end. They had their legs spread apart and were aiming machine guns directly at our windshield.

The rain on the glass was distorting them, twisting their bodies like a funhouse mirror. I braked carefully and eased the car to the right, edging toward the gutter. Then I spun the wheel and made a quick U-turn, heading straight back in the direction of the Lincoln. I heard a horn honk. Gunther lunged out the window, aiming at the other car.

"You stupid bastard!" I shouted to him, but it was too late. A man leaned out of the Lincoln and fired a slim rifle twice, scoring a clean hit on both my front tires. The Jag spun around a hundred eighty degrees and skidded down the road another fifty feet, landing with a ferocious jolt at the base of a sycamore. My head slammed against the roof. Gunther, whose arm was still hanging out the window, was pitched forward. The Magnum flew out of his hand and slid across the asphalt into the swelling river.

We came out with our arms up.

The men from the Lincoln approached us slowly. There were three of them and they were all Latin, wearing slightly tinted glasses and expensive suits that didn't look like they came off a rack. One of them held an umbrella to keep them from getting messed up in the rain. They made us turn around and frisked us quickly, then tied our wrists and pushed us in the back seat of their car. It was upholstered in velvet and had a bar and portable television. Color. The oldest, the one who held the umbrella, had a mouth full of gold fillings. He picked up a telephone between the bucket-style front seats, dialed a number and let out with something in rapid-fire Spanish. The accent wasn't Mexican but I already had a good idea who they were. After a few minutes, they locked the door and took off.

We headed back the way we came, winding our way up Tuna Canyon. I rested my head against the velvet and decided to let it happen, whatever it was going to be.

"Which one of you is Moses Wine?" asked the one with the fillings as we reached the top of a ridge.

"He's Moses Wine. I'm Gunther Thomas, the writer."

The old guy didn't seem impressed. He tapped the driver on the shoulder and we pulled up abruptly at a particularly desolate spot of road.

"*Adios, amigo!*" The one in the back with us threw open the door, grabbed Gunther by the collar and shoved him out of the car. He bounced off a couple of small boulders and into a dense acacia bush.

"You fucking wetbacks!" he yelled, clutching the top of his head.

The Lincoln roared off in the rain.

"That wasn't very nice," I said.

"Where're the tapes?" said the man with the fillings.

"Tapes?"

"You know what I'm talking about."

"What tapes?"

"The *tapes!*" He hit the last word for all it was worth.

"The White House tapes? The milk tapes? The ITT tapes? . . . I'm afraid you've got the wrong man."

He grunted and turned around, punching up the telephone and talking a lot more in rapid-fire Spanish that I couldn't follow.

"Talking to Havana?" I asked. "Oh, I forgot. They kicked you gangsters out fourteen years ago!"

The guy next to me let me have it in the ribs with the butt of his rifle. I was going to ask him where we were going, but I figured I'd get knuckles for an answer so I kept quiet for a while instead.

We headed down the Coast Highway, driving at the limit, and up the ramp onto the Santa Monica Freeway. My companion in the back switched on the television, watching the end of a soap opera on KMEX, the Spanish-language station. That was followed by a commercial in which a dealer from Pacoima auctioned off a used Mercury convertible; then there was a rerun of last week's soccer game from Bolivia.

By the time they reached the second half, we were rounding the interchange onto the Harbor Freeway in downtown L.A. Five minutes later I started to get an inkling of where we were going and I didn't like it. It was almost five o'clock and the kids would be home soon.

"Listen, fellows, what are you trying to pull?" I said, as we pulled up in front of my house. The blinds were drawn and there was a strange car parked in the driveway — a vintage T-Bird, license plate: REGRESO.

They didn't bother to answer, yanking me out of the car and pushing me up to my own front door.

"Santiago?" said the one with the fillings.

"*Abierto.*"

He opened the door.

I felt a sudden rush of blood. Simon was on the babysitter's lap in the middle of the living room floor with Jacob right beside her. They were all staring at the barrel of a .45 revolver held by a tall, ugly man with a hairlip, who had the chamber out spinning. I guessed Santiago was the dark, handsome man in his forties wearing an art deco sport shirt and sitting in my easy chair smoking a small cigar. He got up and greeted us warmly.

"How do you do, Mr. Wine? My name is Santiago Martin . . . I hope I haven't inconvenienced you."

"You have my two small children and one personal friend five feet away from the barrel of a gun. Call off your man or I'll kill you."

"A mere display." He snapped his fingers and the other man tossed him the gun. "It is not loaded . . . see." He showed me the slugs in his hand. "Why don't you sit down and try to calm yourself, Mr. Wine."

He pointed to the sofa. I did as he said. Simon got up and ran over, burying his head in my chest. Jacob followed him over and sat down beside me, taking my arm. I admired his aplomb, would have been proud of it if I wasn't so furious.

"There is nothing to fear. You have such nice children. Your older boy is a good basketball player. I saw him at

54

school." He sat down in my easy chair. "I think there has been some confusion . . . a mix-up."

"I hope so."

He extinguished his cigar and smiled at the babysitter. Her lips were trembling and I had never seen her so white. She was a shy girl, a sociology student at City College, and I hated to get her into this kind of thing.

Santiago turned back to me. "No doubt you have heard of the suicide of this journalist . . . Jock Hecht."

"Yeah, I heard about it."

"I read in the morning papers how you were the one who discovered the body."

I nodded.

"You found a note admitting he murdered the television announcer Deborah Frank."

"There was a note."

"Did you find anything else?"

There was a menacing edge to his voice. I put my arm around Jacob and held Simon down with my free hand. The others drew closer behind Santiago. I felt like pulling the trap out from under them so they'd all fall into a pit full of crocodiles.

"What do you mean?"

"There's a little matter of some tapes."

"What tapes?"

"Tapes that were in the possession of Hecht until his apparent suicide."

"Where are they now?"

"Missing."

"How do you know?"

He looked at the others. "I know."

"Where did he keep these tapes?"

"In the bottom file cabinet to the right."

"Those cabinets were locked."

"Anybody could get into them." His voice rose slightly. "At ten twenty-five this morning they were completely empty . . . Where are those tapes, Mr. Wine?"

55

"I have no idea."

"You must have them . . . unless you have already returned them to El Jefe."

"Who's El Jefe?"

Santiago stared at me. "Let's not play games, Mr. Wine."

"I'm for that. Let's level. I was working for Hecht to clear him of the Deborah Frank murder. I went back to his bungalow so I could ask him some questions when I discovered him dead. A few minutes later his wife arrived from New York and I called the police. I never saw any tapes. I never heard of any tapes. You've got the wrong man, so please get out of my house."

He smiled and turned to Jacob. "What does your boy think?"

Jacob looked up at me. I could see he wanted to talk. Simon was clutching at my chest, making noises like Bambi. These bastards knew how to put it in the lowest possible way. They had years of experience.

"Look," I said. "Suppose something else happened? Suppose Hecht was murdered? Suppose the person who murdered him took the tapes?"

"Then who killed Deborah Frank? It makes no sense."

I had no answer for that one.

"And if he was murdered," Santiago went on, "it would have been to avenge her death. The murderer would have known nothing about the tapes." He stood up. "Mr. Wine, you are wasting our time . . . Where are the tapes?"

"I don't have them, Mr. Martin."

"You are sure of that?"

"Yes."

"Absolutely?"

I nodded.

He breathed in deeply and sighed, then turned to the hairlip with the automatic and started rattling away in Spanish. But his was much easier to follow. I could catch some of the words like *muchachos* and *llevar* — "children" and "take out." I think he wanted me to understand.

56

"Wait a minute, Mr. Martin . . . I'll try to find your tapes. I'll try to get them for you. Just give me some time."

He took out one of his small cigars and fired it up, the flame jumping high off the end as he puffed. "All right, Señor Wine, I'll give you some time. Forty-eight hours."

"But you'll have to tell me what's supposed to be on them."

He laughed. "Come now."

"How many are there?"

"There are three. They are Memorex cassettes with the dates May 3, 4 and 5, 1970 written on them in black ink." And with that he signaled the others he was ready to leave. "*Adios, chico,*" he said to Jacob, ruffling his hair. "You have good hands and you're fast . . . Don't forget, Mr. Wine — forty-eight hours." He shut the door behind them.

The bastards, I thought, the slimy bastards. I watched them through the curtains as they slowly drove off; first the Lincoln, then Santiago's T-Bird. When they were gone, I reached for the phone to call a cab. But there was no tone. It had been disconnected.

10

"You're a crazy lady. Seventy-six years old and out here in the rain. I've been looking all over for you. What're you doing?"

"You don't read?" She pointed up at the placard she was carrying. It was in Yiddish.

"I'm a little rusty."

"I'll translate for the illiterate younger generation — FIGHT SEXISM AMONG THE ORTHODOX. A MINYAN MEANS MEN AND WOMEN! You know what's a *minyan*?"

I nodded. "Ten Jews."

"You know what's sexism?"

"Yeah."

She looked at me doubtfully. We were standing out in front of the Beth David Synagogue, an Orthodox *shul* near the corner of Fairfax and Olympic. A stooped Hasidic Jew walked past. Sonya Levinson waved her placard proudly in the air. He gave her a dirty look and spit at the curb. "*Shmendrik!*" she hissed after him.

When he was out of sight, I pulled her under the synagogue doorway. "Aunt Sonya, I'm in trouble . . . deep trouble . . . Some Cuban *gusanos* want to snatch my kids."

"No? . . . How'd that happen?"

58

"It's too complicated to explain. I'm not even sure myself . . . I want you to take care of them for a while."

"Not around here. The place is crawling with Cubans . . . Why don't you ask your Mexican lady?"

"She's gone." I waved off into the distance, a note of finality in my voice. "Look, I have someplace else in mind. Someplace with good security . . . You'll need some money." I took out my wallet and counted a hundred and sixty dollars, all the cash I had in the house. "If you need more, write a check. I'll reimburse you."

"Where are they?"

I nodded up the block where the cab was hugging the curb. Jacob had his face pressed to the rear window. Simon was already asleep in the back seat, curled in a fetal ball, next to a suitcase full of one-day-old tee shirts, some Charlie Brown books and Jacob's Bruce Lee button collection.

"Jacob," I said through the open door, "don't forget to finish your reading workbook. And remind Simon to tell Aunt Sonya when he has to go shit."

Jacob nodded gravely and I stepped aside for Sonya.

"Where we going?" she asked, positioning herself next to the children.

"Disneyland."

"What! . . . I'm not —"

"Hurray!" said Jacob. I thought he would like that for a hide-out.

I slammed the door shut and leaned in the driver's window. "Take these people to Disneyland," I told him, turning back to Sonya before she could muster a protest. "Check into the Disneyland Hotel and stay there until you hear from me. Take the kids to the amusement park if you want, but keep close to the security guards. They're all over the place. That's why I picked it."

I kissed both boys good-bye, slammed the door and thumped on the back of the cab. They drove off. It wasn't until then that I remembered Sonya didn't have any extra clothes. But that didn't matter. She always wore the same

59

babushka anyway. And the same ratty sweater. It was a gift from Trotsky.

I started hiking up Fairfax. It was already past eight and I needed to rent a car. The Jag could stay where it was for a while, another abandoned wreck in Topanga. I only had forty-eight hours, or forty-seven, or forty-six and a half or whatever was still left.

I found an Avis at a motel off Beverly and killed another twenty minutes waiting for the car to be delivered. It was a new Comet with a stick shift and a radio that screeched when you touched the dial. It took me five minutes to get going because I forgot it wouldn't start until the safety belt was hooked. When I finally got untracked, I headed straight for the Chateau Marmont.

When I got to Hecht's bungalow, the reporters had gone, but the reggae band next door was still going full blast. What was a suicide to deter them? They had a steel drummer who could go day and night and enough dope to turn on a rock festival. I knocked on Hecht's door. Nancy opened it without delay. She was wearing a yellow peignoir buttoned to the neck, a tall glass of brandy in her hand. The way I was feeling, I took one look at her green eyes and wanted to fall on top of her, burying my head in her stomach. But I walked past coolly instead, continuing on into the living room. She followed me in.

"How've you been?" I asked.

"Not so good . . . What about you?"

"Not so good either. Some refugees put a little pressure on me and my kids."

I looked down at the file cabinet. One of the drawers had been broken into all right, the bottom one on the right-hand side. It seemed to have been pried out with a crowbar from the bottom. A few folders filled with tax receipts had spilled over in the back.

Nancy walked over to the desk. "It happened this morning," she said, "when I was at your home. I tried to reach you all afternoon but your phone's been out of order."

60

"Yeah, I know . . . Did you tell the police?"

"No. Why should I tell them? They'd just muck it up."

I agreed, but it sounded strange coming from her. I looked at her awhile, then poured myself a drink and told her about the Cubans. She was sympathetic about the kids, but she didn't know anything about Santiago Martin or any tapes.

"You think they could have killed him themselves," she suggested, "and taken the tapes? Maybe they're trying to use you as an alibi."

"Anything is possible. I can't make connections. Did Jock ever tell you about an Institute, the Liberation Institute?"

She shook her head.

"Or the League? The Sexual Liberation League?"

"No."

I sipped on the drink and walked over to the desk. She watched me curiously as I opened the bottom drawer and took out the journal, flipping through the pages again. An early entry caught my eye:

> Anyone of us is capable of sex with anything — man, woman or beast. Conventional wisdom is that we must ward it off, distort our nature in order to preserve civilization. I say — ridiculous! I'd stick it in a dead lizard if it pleased me.

I thought that one over for a second, then went on, glancing over the entries for a clue. None of the names seemed likely, all either normal business contacts for a writer — editors, agents, promoters — or references to dead philosophers not likely to help in solving our case. I stared at the first page again when Nancy came up behind me, looking over my shoulder. I could feel her breasts brushing against my back.

"Find anything interesting?"

"Not unless you're hot for lizards."

"Are you?"

"I ate an iguana once, but I wouldn't want to fuck one."

I turned back and looked at her. She was smiling, placing her empty glass on the table and sliding around the front of

61

the sofa. "Have you ever tried?" she asked.

"No."

"Then you shouldn't prejudge the experience."

"I never met an iguana who was in the mood."

"Iguanas have to be approached carefully . . . taken by surprise."

I walked over to her. She was looking at me, her head cocked to one side, her hand resting over the arm of the sofa. Outside, someone slammed a door. I could hear laughter and shouting, Dan Hick's band on a stereo doing "Midnight at the Oasis." I reached down and slid my fingers along the sofa, touching the back of her hand. She didn't move.

"I think you've got the wrong idea," she said.

"About what?"

"Open marriage . . . It doesn't work that way. You don't sleep with everyone just because you're free to do it."

"I didn't think you would."

At that moment Gunther burst in, followed by a tall girl dressed like Carmen Miranda and three other revellers from the party next door. His head was bandaged from the nasty fall and he was pushing a tank of nitrous oxide.

"What's this?" he said very slowly. You could tell they'd been taking gas. "A new duo for Joyce Haber? Author's aggrieved widow and dope-smoking shamus!" He sucked on the nitrous and started holding his sides.

"Glad to see you back, Gunther."

"No thanks to you, pal. I hitched a ride with some leather freaks and made it to Cindy's in time for the Sensory Awareness Seminar. She fixed me up fine after it was over." He smiled mischievously. A skinny dude in a sequined blouse and bleached orange hair grabbed for the hose, but Gunther held tight, twisting the valve open with a silver wrench and giving himself a huge dose. The others circled around ominously. Gas made you greedy, but I wouldn't have minded a big hit myself.

"She wanted me to lead a group bath. Can you imagine?" he went on, coming out of it. "I declined, man. Deadlines.

We've got to have the copy on the Mojo wire by closing Wednesday night, and I can't rely on some addle-brained, acid-damaged gumshoe to solve this case for me. He can't even find fucking Meiko."

"There is no Meiko."

"Says who?"

"Hecht called everyone Meiko."

"You want to bet?" Gunther focused on one of the revellers, a curly-haired, greying man trying to look Beverly Hillship in faded jeans and a Twentieth Century Fox tee shirt. "This man here, Sal Gruskow, knows all about Meiko. She was the star of one of his movies."

"Not the star," said Gruskow. He sounded like a 78 record played on 33-1/3. "Just a girl that got fucked along the way. It was a Kung Fu horror movie called *The Blood Leeches of Dr. Wu*."

"You sure we're talking about the same girl?" I asked him.

"Sure I'm sure. Meiko. The one that works at the Kama Sutra Sexual Phrontistery."

"Then Rhonda lied."

"What?"

"Never mind."

"Well, that's where she works and that's, uh, where I discovered her."

"Where can I find her?"

"She's doing another picture for me right now. *The Badass Brigade*. It's a Civil War, black-exploitation movie. Sort of the flip side of *Gone with the Wind*."

"Where is she right now?"

"Well, we're not on location until Wednesday. Tomorrow she should still be at the Phrontistery. But if you don't find her there, call me at the studio and I'll see what I can do about it."

He wedged his fingers in his tight jeans and pulled out his card. I stuffed it in my shirt and turned to look for Nancy. But she wasn't there. She wasn't in the kitchen either. I was about to start up the stairs when Gunther zipped across the room and stole the nitrous out of Gruskow's hands. "Goal to goal!" he shouted, hunching over the tank and running it around the bungalow like a fullback breaking ahead of the field. The others chased him like linebackers, trying to make a last-minute lunge at his ankles. They ran around the living room twice before he tripped, vaulting over the coffee table, and they surrounded him. But he bounced up, faking right, and dove through the bathroom door, locking it behind him. Inside, we could hear him sucking on the mouthpiece and giggling hysterically. It sounded like a side trip to Loon Lake at midnight.

The revellers sagged and started back for their bungalow. I checked my watch. It was nine forty-five. I took a last look around downstairs and climbed up to the balcony. I found Nancy in the bedroom. She was stretched out on the sheets, her head buried in the pillow, crying. I started to back out.

"No, it's all right," she said, sitting up.

"What's wrong?"

"Nothing."

"Nothing?"

"I'm okay!"

"You're not okay. You were crying."

She shrugged. "Don't you cry?"

"Is it Jock?"

"I don't know. Everything."

"What else?"

"Nothing else."

"Look, I try to tell you what happens. You ought to level with me."

"What do you want me to tell you?" she asked.

There was a loud crash from below followed by a series of high-pitched giggles resembling the tittering of baby monkeys.

"We better get him out," I said.

Nancy nodded and took a key from under the headboard. We went downstairs and she unlocked the bathroom door. Gunther was asleep on the floor, a beautiful grin spread across his face.

When he came out of it, I pulled him up and helped him out the front door, then turned back to Nancy, who was leaning against the jamb.

"What are you trying to say?" she asked, staring at me steadily. The neon sign of the Marmont cast an orange glow across her face.

"It's about open marriage. What if one of the partners gets hung up on someone they're playing around with. Doesn't that create problems?"

"You have to watch out for that." She waited a beat, then turned away from me. "Good night," she said, and bolted shut the door.

I walked past the party. The reggae band was taking an intermission. A blonde woman was vomiting on the steps while one of the musicians patted her on the back.

I got into the car and drove home along Hollywood Boulevard, staring out at the passing parade of the nighttime city. It was a depressing sight. Even in the rain, the streets were lined with leathery whores and fourteen-year-old transvestites, six-foot black glitter queens in torn, gold stockings and feather boas. The whole society had gone decadent, but without style — a Weimar Republic with no cabarets and no George Grosz to draw it.

I drove home in the rain feeling depressed and apprehensive. I hoped Gruskow had given me a lead on Meiko. I sure needed it.

I parked the car in the driveway and walked to the front door. The lights were out as I reached for the key under the rubber tree. Inside, the place was quiet, empty, like it had been before Suzanne left the country and the kids lived with her. It unnerved me. I thought of the kids in the Disneyland Hotel and started to get paranoid. What if those Cuban bastards had already found them there and broken into their room, holding them at gunpoint? What kind of father was I, fifty miles north in Echo Park, leaving all that responsibility in Sonya's hands? So she fought the czar's dragoons on the steps of the Winter Palace at the age of fourteen; what if she had escaped a Stalinist Labor Camp and crossed Siberia in bare feet to join the Yugoslav resistance; even if . . . she was still seventy-six years old. Seventy-six years old and recently hospitalized at Cedars-Sinai for pleurisy.

I sat down on the bed and lit up a joint to get ahold of myself. Tomorrow I had a job to do. I took a few solid hits and put it out. I slipped under the covers and tried to masturbate. But it wouldn't come. I was too nervous, my mind too scattered. I concentrated on various women I knew — on Alora, even Suzanne — but it didn't help. Then Nancy Hecht came into my mind. Pale-skinned, semiliberated Nancy. Nancy the teacher. Nancy the fair.

I slept well after that.

The next morning at ten I was parked along a side street behind the Kama Sutra Sexual Phrontistery. I had stopped off briefly to cash a check and it was early, but the massage parlor didn't appear to be drawing much business. I waited five minutes, watching the building. From a sign in the window I could see a new wrinkle had been added to the parlor's list of offerings — Half & Half Massage. "You massage me and I massage you. We learn from each other. $35 a half hour." At least the prices weren't going up.

A paunchy businessman drove up to the front door in a Toyota, took a quick look at the place and changed his mind. It was a credit to his taste. After he had driven off, I got out and circled around the back. I wanted to find a rear door and enter without Rhonda seeing me, if it were possible, then search discretely among the rooms for Meiko.

There weren't any ground-level doors, but there was a trap on the side which led to a cellar underneath the Phrontistery. I slithered down and passed through some storage rooms filled with faded travel posters and outdated brochures for group excursions to Nicaragua and Guatemala, then found a back stairway — but it went nowhere. I retraced my steps to an abandoned kitchen, pushed through the swinging door and entered. It had obviously been unused for some time. There was a decrepit stove and dumbwaiter near an icebox. I stuck my head inside the dumbwaiter. The platform was gone but there was a rope and the chute seemed to be free and clear to the main floor.

At the top, the door was locked. It was made of cheap pasteboard, and I tried to pry it open without forcing too hard and creating a disturbance. But my fist slipped, smashing the pasteboard and sending the door crashing to the floor with a loud bang. I thought I would be discovered the instant I stuck my head through the opening, but pandemonium had already broken out. A siren was wailing, screaming through the windows, as five prowl cars pulled up at the front of the Phrontistery followed by a paddywagon, an anti-riot crew, two mobile units from local television and a black Eldorado limousine with the state flag on it. It was the biggest goddamn vice raid I had ever seen, an incredible piece of overkill, like using the entire Chinese Army to capture South Pasadena. And all I could see coming out of the place were three terrified topless masseuses and one scaly kid with a towel around his waist who couldn't have been more than nineteen.

I ducked back into the dumbwaiter, descended and slid out quickly, running around the front of the building to watch. The cops were already out of their cars and were led by Koontz, who was having a hard time with Rhonda.

"Come on, sergeant, why're you picking on us? . . . We're the smallest place on the block!"

"Relax, sister, you were overdue for a raid six months ago."

"What about the League? Why don't you hit the League places? They do everything we do!"

"Keep your shirt on, lady. We know what we're doing. The League is next. They're right on the list." He waved a clipboard at her.

"The hell they are! I'll believe it when I see it!"

A cameraman from KNXT dropped to his knees for a close-up of Rhonda giving Koontz the Bronx cheer when a group of big shots in grey suits and white shoes got out of the El-

dorado and walked directly toward the cameras. I recognized Phil Warren from the Board of Supervisors, City Attorney Bart Lipsky and none other than Frank Dichter, Attorney General of the State of California. Dichter was a tall,
big-shouldered man with sandy grey hair he had only recently grown longer than a brush cut. I was surprised to see him
all the way down here, but everyone knew Dichter had his
eye on the governor's mansion up in Sacramento. This was
the kind of exposure he could use.

He frowned for the folks at home as the girls were herded
into the paddywagon. I searched among them for an Oriental, but couldn't find any. No Meiko. Down to my right, the
scaly kid was doing a quick plea, bargaining with one of the
policemen, clutching determinedly to his towel. I watched him
squirm as Koontz and one of the other cops cut a path
through the gathering crowd for the Attorney General, the
flacks following close behind him like lemmings.

"Call me unsophisticated," said Dichter, turning to the reporters for an impromptu press conference, "but the trouble
with this state is that we've turned soft on sex. I don't mean
what goes on between consenting adults in the privacy of
their own homes. This is 1974 and that's their affair. But
this flagrant public display — this obvious prostitution mas-
querading as physical therapy — corrupts the minds of our
children and weakens the public will to push this country
forward in a time of grave international crisis. This must
cease. Indeed we are remiss for not having wiped it out
years ago."

An assistant in a Gatsby sweater came forward. "Do any
of you gentlemen and ladies have a question for the Attorney General?"

Several hands went up. Dichter pointed to a well-dressed
woman with a poodle cut.

"Lynn Lipman from KNBC. I'd like to ask the Attorney
General if he thinks there's a danger in drawing such a fine
line between closing these establishments and repressing the
freedom of the individual?"

"A good question, miss. We've given a great deal of thought to this problem and a committee in my office will be issuing its report shortly."

He pointed to another hand.

"Pete DeBretteville, the Hollywood *Citizen News*. I'd like to know if you have any plans to move in on *Deep Throat*?"

"I'm afraid these decisions are in the hands of your local law enforcement officials." Dichter turned and smiled icily in the direction of the City Attorney. "But if you ask me, I say there are no half measures."

My hand shot in the air.

"Bill Mays, Glendale *Tribune*. Our sources tell us there's been resistance to investigating massage parlors belonging to the League."

"The League?"

"Yes. Would you care to comment?"

"I don't know what you're talking about."

"The Sexual Liberation League. They control the largest chain of massage parlors in West Hollywood."

"I'm not familiar with what companies hold this kind of place. Every place like it will be equally treated."

"Well, our sources say there might even be a whitewash in the making."

"A whitewash?" He hesitated for a moment. "Well, now, we'll have to look into this. What paper did you say you were with?"

"The Glendale *Tribune*."

Dichter turned to his assistant and whispered to him.

"He's not with the Glendale *Tribune*," said a voice behind me. "His name is Moses Wine and he's a private detective." Koontz blew my cover.

I took a step back. Dichter gritted his teeth and smiled fatuously at the others. "Well, well. We've reached a new level of investigative journalism. Private detectives questioning public officials at press conferences. I hope this doesn't create a backlash." He turned to Koontz. "What's the next stop on our itinerary, sergeant?"

Koontz pointed up the street. "The Sexual Cafeteria."

"Then let's go," said Dichter, leading his entourage in the direction Koontz had pointed. "Perhaps they're a member of this League." He turned back to me with a look of cold fury, then headed off down the street.

Koontz grabbed me by the arm. "Get a little brains in your pinko skull, Winegold . . . It's all the League." He motioned at the row of massage parlors. "If it ain't in the League, it ain't."

He followed Dichter off. I lingered by the curb for a few seconds, watching him. A couple of policemen were chucking the Phrontistery paraphernalia out onto the street — some purple cushions, strings of beads, bottles of oils, a deflated waterbed. Another was taking down the sign, the nauseating version of Botticelli's Venus, to reveal an old travel agency sign underneath. It's name, "Viajes Miami" in flaming letters, surprised me, but not half as much as the name of its director printed in a small script at the bottom — Santiago Martin.

11

Eleven thirty. There were only about thirty hours left before I had to confront Santiago, and I still knew next to nothing — at least nothing that made sense. No Meiko. No tapes. No Hecht murder. No Deborah Frank. I was barreling out Olympic, heading west and running out of gas. I considered stopping but the lines were long so I went on, passing the Avenue of the Stars and turning right into the Fox lot.

Gruskow's name got me by the gate. I drove slowly through the *Hello, Dolly* set, its false Victorian front rising up against the glass façades of Century City. I found the producer's office behind the antiseptic plaza where years ago they had filmed *Peyton Place*. When I went inside, Gruskow was in the middle of a story conference.

"All right, terrific," he said, beckoning me through the door. "Now we can settle this. We have an expert witness!"

I walked past the receptionist into his office. It was modishly furnished with a lucite desk and a discussion area held an aluminum chair and sofa beneath an Ed Ruscha lithograph. Gruskow was there with Lars Gundersen, a middle-aged Swedish director, and Matt Zimmerman, a kid who looked around twenty-two and was introduced as the screenwriter.

"Here's the situation," said Gruskow. "Lars writes me

from Sweden and says, Sal, the time has come for me to make a picture in America and I want to make it with you. Great, I think, and call him straight away, person-to-person, at his villa in Malmö. What do you want to do, Lars? I ask. A gangster film, he says, like you used to make them in the forties, like *White Heat* or *High Sierra*. Great, I say, I have just the writer for you." They looked over at Zimmerman who appeared a little uneasy. "Fine, he says, let's go. So Fox fronts the money and flies Lars over and here we are. Trouble is, we can't get a handle on it."

The receptionist leaned in the door. "Bart Cohen is on the line."

"Hold the calls, Florence . . . So that's the story. We're here to make a gangster picture, but we don't have a plot."

"They've all been done," said Gundersen. "Your police, your dope addicts, your Manson and those hippies."

"Any new angles?" asked Gruskow. "You're a detective."

"I came here to find Meiko."

"Meiko? . . . You said a dirty word!"

"She wasn't at the Phrontistery."

"You're telling me? We've been looking for her all morning. *Badass* has had a change in shooting schedule. Florence got her home address from the business office. Meiko's landlady hasn't seen her since Friday. It's a mess. We're going to have to reshoot two days."

That was all I needed to hear. I checked my watch. Eleven fifty-five. The time was ticking away.

Gruskow looked at me. "Come on, Wine. Be a *mensch*. You must have bumped into some pretty strange types."

"I had this idea for an existential approach to the Mafia," said Gundersen, "but —"

"But how many Mafia movies can you make in a year," said Gruskow, growing impatient.

"What about Jewish crooks?" I asked. "They ought to be due for a raking over."

"Hey, I like that," said Zimmerman.

"Oh, Christ, no," said the producer. "The studio would

never go along."

"Why not?"

"I know how they think. This is a Jewish industry. They're not going to attack their own kind. Besides, some of the old studio chiefs were related to the gangsters. How do you think they got their distribution? It was *mishpocheh*."

"You mean like Bugsy Siegel?" said Zimmerman, wide-eyed.

"Yeah, yeah. Arnold Rothstein, Meyer Lansky, the whole Kosher Nostra."

"Who else?" I asked.

"Oh, you know . . ."

"Meyer Greenglass?" I suggested.

"Yeah. Him."

"Who was he related to?"

"Oh, Christ . . . I forget." Gruskow snapped his fingers in the air.

"Max Frank?"

"Yeah, that's right . . . old Maxie Frank at Allied Studios. Greenglass married his sister Lotte back in . . . Hey, where're you going?"

"To jail," I said and ran out the door.

12

So Meyer Greenglass was Debbie Frank's uncle. Now, if a man like Greenglass thought Hecht killed his niece, he would have had him hit in a minute. It all made sense. Or kind of. If you didn't try to fit the Cubans into it, or the tapes, or the Sexual Liberation League. Of course, Greenglass could have had connections to Cuba before Castro. A little side action in the casinos. The tapes might update that story. And as for sexual liberation, I'm sure Meyer was no prude, especially when there was money involved. But why were the Cubans looking for the tapes? And where the hell was Meiko?

I sped down the Harbor Freeway to Terminal Island, keeping one eye on the speedometer and the other on the gas gauge. The former was erratic, the latter was hovering at zero and heading down. Pretty soon I would be driving on spit. I slowed down and coasted, coming off the bridge onto the island, then rolled the next few blocks past the tuna cannery to the federal prison. I reached the gate at twenty minutes past one.

Greenglass wouldn't see me. This wasn't a good time. He was having his semi-annual check-up at the prison hospital, then taking his afternoon nap. When would be a good time, I asked, sending word through the same guard as on my first visit. This time he didn't even bother to answer.

74

I sat down and wrote him a letter:

Dear Meyer,

Since you were not exactly forthright with me concerning your relationship to Deborah Frank, I remain suspicious of your complicity in the death of Jock Hecht. Further investigation leads me to believe a group of Cuban refugees and a holding company called the Sexual Liberation League are involved in this affair as well as some tapes missing from Hecht's files. If you do not comment on or explain your role in this within the next *twelve hours*, I shall be obliged to inform the police. I may be reached at home (380-0466) or at Nancy Hecht's bungalow at the Chateau Marmont.

Sincerely,
Moses Wine

I sealed the letter in an envelope and handed it to the guard. Then I left the prison and drove to the end of the first gas line I could find, turned off the engine and slipped into a phone booth to call the Disneyland Hotel.

"Tante Sonya, this is Moses. How are things?"

"Things are all right, except the children are really missing you, Moses. Jacob woke up last night and watched television with me. *Top Hat* with Fred Astaire. He knows it by heart, so I couldn't get him back to sleep for three hours."

"How's Simon?"

"Fine. He's banging on a piano. The hotel was booked up so they stuck us up in the penthouse suite. It's got a concert grand piano, painted white."

"Wonderful. How's security?"

"Well, that's the problem . . ."

"Hold on a second." I let the receiver dangle while I ran outside and inched my car forward in the line toward the pump. "Now, how's the security?"

"I was going to tell you. This suite, they don't have a corridor. You take the elevator straight up into the living room.

75

They could come straight up past the guards."

"Change rooms."

"I'm trying . . . And today, when we were in Disneyland, this strange man was following us onto Mr. Toad's Ride. At least I think he was following us. Maybe he was Cuban. I don't know."

"What happened?"

A woman in a Dodge was honking for me to advance my car again.

"Nothing. Nothing happened."

"Don't worry," I said, gritting my teeth. "Maybe he was one of those sexists trying to make a pass at you."

"Very funny." The woman in the Dodge was still honking. An angry pump attendant was heading in my direction. "You want to talk to the children?"

"I can't. We'd just get depressed . . . Keep in touch." I hung up, feeling guilty as hell.

I filled the tank and headed back to the Marmont. The rain was persisting into its second day now, leaving a fine sheen on the freeways — and several accidents. L.A. drivers were lousy in the rain; they weren't used to it. When it came, they drove foolishly, skidding and sliding all over hell. It wasn't a day to take risks. A mudslide had already closed the Foothill Freeway in Sylmar.

The weather had even dampened the reggae party by the time I reached the Marmont. The last of the partygoers was out front, yelling to a bellboy about a leak in the kitchen. Nancy's bungalow had a leak too, or at least an incipient one. A large, grey stain was spreading like damp fungus across the ceiling of the two-story living room when I entered.

"You're going to have a waterfall in a minute," I told her and went into the kitchen for some pots.

"They don't seem to build for the long-term around here," she said.

"It's a Moorish tradition. The Spaniards brought it with them to California. The Moors always figured if you don't build for rain, it won't rain."

"What'd they think about earthquakes?"

She looked at me for a second. It was clear she wasn't interested in the answer.

"Any news?" she asked, after I stationed three pots and a coffee cup strategically on the floor.

"Yeah, something surprising. I found out Meyer Greenglass was Deborah Frank's uncle."

Her face went white and she sank into an armchair.

"What's wrong?"

"Nothing . . . What does it mean?"

"That he had a damn good reason to kill Jock, better than the credit card nonsense. And he's the kind of man who would do it in a minute. There are still a lot of pieces that don't come together — like the tapes and the Cubans and the League — but we'll figure it out. I left a message for Greenglass to call within twelve hours or I'd go to the police. My guess is we'll be hearing from him soon."

"You think so?"

The phone rang. I looked at Nancy with a complacent smile on my face. She reached for the receiver.

"Hello, bungalow five . . . This is Nancy Hecht speaking." She turned to me. "It's for you."

"Is it Greenglass?"

"It's a woman."

I shrugged and took the phone from her, kicking one of the pots under the first drop of water. "Hello, this is Moses Wine."

"Hello, Moses, this is Cynthia Hardwick."

"Hello, Dr. Hardwick. Are you all right? You sound woozy."

"I guess so . . . I just came to. There's been some trouble."

"What happened?"

"I was in my office at the Institute when I heard someone at the shredding machine. I went in to see who it was and he hit me on the head. I must have passed out."

"Where is he now?"

"I don't know."

"You still there?"

"Uh huh."

"I'll be right over."

I hung up and started for the door when I saw Nancy putting on the serape. "I'm coming with you," she said.

She followed me across the pool and down to the car. We jumped in and sped over Laurel Canyon, catching the Ventura Freeway to Topanga. The rain was coming down in buckets now; a VW camper in front of us was doing a fishtail. The clouds were so dense you couldn't even see the McDonald's stands on Victory Boulevard.

I pulled off at Topanga and drove faster than I should up the north end of the canyon. Traffic was light and I was making good time until we were forced to stop at the top where the police had set up a roadblock to keep traffic off the canyon floor. A highway patrol officer approached us, wearing a plastic-coated hat and yellow slicker.

"Sorry, folks, can't go through. This is a slide area."

"What?"

"Residents of the canyon only."

"We're residents of the canyon," I said.

"May I see some identification?"

I hesitated. "We're long-term visitors staying up at the Liberation Institute."

He gave me a suspicious look.

"You ever heard of the Institute?"

"Yeah." He sounded as if I had mentioned a leper colony.

"We only visit for about a week at a time."

"You still need proof!"

"We do?" Nancy smiled the best she could.

"But what about that guy?" I pointed to the car behind us.

He turned and I spun the wheel, swerving to the right and speeding around the roadblock. In seconds we had passed the bend and were a hundred yards down the road. There was no way they could catch us until we came out the other end.

Soon we were down by the shopping center. I turned up Fernwood, looking for the tributary road at the top. I found the sign and headed down the dark road, live oaks and the storm clouds blocking out what was left of the twilight sun. To my right, the dry river was swollen. It seemed almost like a Colorado rapid. A sheer cliff dropped off on the other side, a few yards ahead of where my old Jag was wedged in a ditch beyond the empty ranch house. We continued by without incident to the gate of the Institute.

The Liberation Institute was marked by a large wooden placard over a chain link fence. The driveway was wider than the main road itself and led past a swimming pool, tennis courts, what appeared to be guest houses and through an expansive lawn to the main building at the top. This was an imposing edifice built in an improbable Tyrolean style with dark shingles and a cantilevered overhanging roof. The surrounding grounds had been elaborately landscaped with azaleas and delphiniums and meticulously-clipped hedges. The whole place reminded me of a Swiss sanitarium for the wealthy disturbed.

We drove around the side to the parking lot and got out. It was filled with expensive cars — Mercedes, Lincolns, Cadillacs and Maseratis. The walkways were paved with marble and the front door was made of bronze with a frieze of a naked couple in the missionary position. You had to be pretty well-heeled to take your liberation in a place like this. We rang the bell and a peephole appeared in the left breast of the woman on the door.

"Who is it?" It was a man's voice.

"Moses Wine. I'm here to see Dr. Hardwick."

"One moment, please."

The breast slid shut. We waited a few moments until the door was opened by a naked man in his thirties with a slight gut and a La Cienega men's salon haircut. In the outside world he might have been a PR man or an advertising executive. Behind him, several couples were seated on a Persian rug on the living room floor, fondling each other by the roaring fire.

"Hi, I'm Charlie," he said, extending his hand to us as we came inside. "I'm one of the facilitators . . . You'll have to take your clothes off. House rules."

He pointed to a changing room with no door. I walked in ahead of Nancy and started to undress. She stood by the entrance, unsure of what to do.

"You should be used to this," I said.

She mumbled something and turned away, staring off at a bookshelf. It was lined with weighty treatises on sex by writers like Havelock Ellis and Wilhelm Reich. She walked up to it, fingering the volumes, pulling one out and stuffing it back in again. Then she sat down and began thumbing through some of the magazines on the bottom shelf.

"You wanted to come, didn't you?"

She nodded and walked over to the side wall, undressing slowly with her back to me. I watched her out of the corner of my eye. You weren't supposed to do that, I knew. You were supposed to accept nudity casually in a place like this. But I watched anyway. Casually. I imagine everybody else did too.

Nancy took off her blouse, then bent over and slipped out of her panties. From behind she looked fine, a firm, mature ass and thin thighs. There was a light brown birthmark right in the middle of her coccyx. I heard her take a deep breath before she turned around. She was no disappointment.

"You can stick your valuables in these," said Charlie, handing us a couple of muslin bags silk-screened with the R. Cobb ecology symbol. I put my wallet and keys inside and slung it over my shoulder. In a distant room, I heard the sound of a gong.

"What's that?" I asked Charlie.

"Tantric yoga. The participants sit on the floor in the lotus position staring into each other's eyes and feeding each other sweetmeats until they are overcome with the desire to make love."

I looked over at Nancy. She had folded her arms across

80

her chest. I couldn't tell if it was from modesty or to keep her breasts from bouncing.

Charlie led us down a corridor past some seminar rooms and a bulletin board which listed Institute activities — a lecture on the polymorphous perverse followed by a pre-dinner Jacuzzi — leaving us by the office at the end. It had an embossed sign reading:

THE LIBERATION INSTITUTE
A WHOLLY OWNED SUBSIDIARY OF
THE SEXUAL LIBERATION LEAGUE OF AMERICA

I opened the door. Cindy was lying on a couch, nursing her jaw with an ice pack. Across the room, I could see another empty file drawer and the paper shredder.

"I'm glad to see you," she said.

"Hello, Cindy. This is Nancy Hecht, Jock's wife ... Nancy, this is Dr. Cynthia Hardwick."

Cindy stood and looked Nancy up and down. "I'm so pleased to meet you. Your husband was such a wonderful man, one of the true bellwethers in the movement to extend mankind's potential for self-expression."

She took Nancy's hand and pressed it to her lips. I felt like throwing up.

"What happened here, Cindy? Why'd you call us?"

"It's exactly as I told you. I was in that seminar room down the hall when I heard someone in here. I opened the door and he knocked me out."

"Did you get a look at him?"

"A quick one. He was a medium-sized man with black hair."

"That's not very helpful. Was he wearing clothes?"

She looked at me strangely.

"Those are your rules here, aren't they? Was he wearing clothes?"

"Yes, of course he was. Khaki pants and a blue sweater. He must have broken in."

"I guess he also got what he was looking for." I motioned

81

toward the file.

She nodded.

"What was he looking for?"

She suddenly got a big pain in her jaw and ducked back behind the ice pack.

"Don't be coy, Cindy. Everything out front, remember?"

"He seems to have taken all the statements and financial records of the League."

"And who *is* the League?"

She didn't say anything. I looked over at the paper shredder. It was a terrifying device with a razor-sharp grid of shining teeth and a plunger that mashed the written word the way those huge vises crush junk cars at wrecking lots. If I were an idol worshipper, I would have bowed down.

"For crissake, Cindy, I'm running out of time! You don't want me to force it out of you."

I turned and gave her my nastiest look. She backed up, afraid of a second knockout.

She spoke softly. "The League is directed by a group of Cubans headed by someone named Santiago Martin. I only met them once, but I wish they would go away."

"So why don't you cut loose?"

"We've tried, but we can't. They own the stock. They're making too much money from us . . . Besides, they don't seem to have a choice. They're only the directors. There's someone behind them. Another investor."

"Who's that?"

"I don't know."

"You sure about that?"

"Yes. It's a silent partner."

"You don't have much of a record for credibility."

"I don't have to —"

She broke off. Down the hall, Charlie and three women were hurrying toward us looking upset. He rushed up to Cindy, grabbing her by the arm and pulling her into the doorway.

"You're not going to believe this!"

"What?"

"Someone's taking pictures!"

"What!"

"In the sauna."

"Oh, my god!"

Cindy threw the ice pack on the floor.

We followed Charlie quickly down another corridor, passing the Jacuzzi and a line of naked people feeding each other bananas, until we arrived at the steam rooms. Charlie pointed toward the glass door. Inside, two men were kissing while a third, sitting opposite, seemingly ignored them. But as they went into a deep embrace, the third man reached into his muslin bag and pulled out a Minox.

"Jesus, it's him!" said Cindy.

"Who?"

"The one at the shredder!"

"I thought he was wearing clothes."

"He must have taken them off!"

I pushed the door open slowly and watched him take a photograph. He was a heavy-set man with a dark moustache and a strawberry mark on his left butt. I slid inside and seated myself next to him on the oak bench. He turned and looked at me.

"Get any good snaps?"

He shoved the camera in the bag and jumped up, heading for the door. I grabbed his wrist, but his skin was sweaty. He slipped through and bolted for the door, running down the corridor. I ran after him, my cock knocking uncomfortably against the inside of my thigh. He was quick for a heavy man and kept eluding me. We trotted through the Jacuzzi and the yoga class into the living room. There was consternation everywhere, people shouting and running around behind the sunken fireplace. He headed for a window along the side, forced it open, took a quick look back and dove, naked, into the pouring rain.

I ran to the window. He was running toward the parking lot. I cut to the front door, Nancy coming up behind me, waving my wallet and car keys.

"Where're you going?" I shouted back at her.

"With you."

"What for?"

But she had no time to answer as I pushed the door open. Across the lot, the man was jumping into a yellow Maverick, his pink skin already specked with mud. We both ran to the Comet, got in and pulled out after him, sliding across the wet cement, following him down the Institute driveway past the swimming pool and the tennis courts. The rain was coming down in torrents, the world wrapped in a heavy gauze. I could barely see him ahead of us as we skidded past the gate of the Institute and sped along the rushing river.

We continued down the road a mile. Two miles. Losing him, catching him. Unable to get closer. Then we began to hear a peculiar, ominous sound, a rumbling noise all around us, growing louder as we drove deeper into the canyon. I didn't like it, but I took a risk and floored the Comet. It flew forward with a screech, jolting us and putting us nearly at the other man's tail. He leaned out the door of his car and fired a gun at us, missing wildly. He was losing ground. The rumbling grew louder, almost deafening. At first I couldn't figure out what it was. I looked over at Nancy. She looked worried too. And frightened, hugging her pale bare skin.

We were bearing down on him now, but the noise, loud as it was, continued to mount. It was reaching cosmic proportions, as if we were standing in the middle of a thunder cloud.

Then we couldn't move. Our wheels were spinning, caught, as if in quicksand. The other car shot ahead, listing right, out of control. The driver screamed and leapt out, a nude figure running in place at the edge of the cliff. Then we were moving again, sideways, heaving toward the cliff.

"What's happening?" said Nancy.

"Slide!"

"What?"

"Jump!"

84

I opened the right hand door and pushed her into the mud, flying out after her, pulling her up and struggling away from the car toward a large hunk of rock, a boulder. Behind us, half the mountain was falling into the river. I heard a blood-curdling scream as we scrambled up the side, skinning and scraping. To our right and below, barely visible through the spraying mud, I could see the naked man riding over the edge of the cliff on a wave of what looked like molten shit.

The two cars followed him.

Then it was quiet.

We stood there in the darkness and rain, our bare feet sunk deep in the wet sand. I couldn't see if Nancy was crying, but I guessed she was because I was. We got down off the rock. I took her hand and we walked along where the road used to be. I didn't know which way. I wasn't thinking about it. We didn't much care.

The wind blew the rain in our faces, whipping around our bare bodies, making us shiver and bending the trees. I kept thinking of an old line from an O. Henry story: "Do the trees moving make the wind blow?" I don't know why. Probably because I had read it as a child and it was comforting. "Do the trees moving make the wind blow?" I said aloud.

"We're going to catch pneumonia," said Nancy.

"Yeah."

"Maybe we should head back for the Institute."

"Uh huh "

"Where is it?"

I stopped and looked around. Nancy was jumping up and down, beating her body with her fists to stay warm. The mudslide had changed the entire landscape, pushing the trunks of trees into the river, even upending some boulders and leaving them in new contortions.

"I think it's that way," I said. "But before we get there, we'll have pneumonia for sure."

"We'd better start anyway."

We started, but after only a few steps, I heard another rumbling noise from up the canyon.

85

"Another slide."

I stopped and tried to think fast. By this time it was pitch dark. We couldn't see more than a few feet ahead without the automobile headlights. And whatever flashlight might have been in the glove compartment was buried under twenty feet of mud.

"There's an old ranch house in the other direction. Let's try that . . ."

We turned back and began walking in the opposite direction. I didn't recognize anything. It was like that old kid's game when you closed your eyes, counted to ten and then opened them again to see if the world had changed.

Then I started to laugh. Here we were, two naked human beings, trudging along in a storm in the middle of nowhere, ready to die of exposure, just because we were stupid enough to chase some idiot who was taking pictures in the sauna of some over-intellectualized exhibitionists. The whole thing was madness.

"What's so funny?" Nancy asked.

"Us."

"I know what you mean."

We laughed together.

"Where'd you go to college?" Nancy asked.

"What?"

"Just making conversation."

"Oh . . . I went to Berkeley."

"I went to Smith . . . What was your major?"

"Major? Major? Oh, English, then I went law school but I couldn't take it."

"I majored in comparative lit. For a while I thought about being a foreign correspondent."

"What happened?"

"I don't know . . . My mother didn't want me to go away from home. She was kind of a strict Catholic."

"Parents . . ." I said, stubbing my toe on a rock. Off in the distance I could hear a horse whinny. "Hey, I think we're getting near the ranch."

Nancy smiled. I looked at her and tripped over a log. We were getting slap-happy.

The door was locked and the lights were out when we finally reached the ranch, but given our situation I wasted no time in throwing a small rock through a front window. Knocking aside some of the glass, I put my foot on the sill and climbed in.

It was a nice, homey little ranch house, probably somebody's weekend retreat from the look of it, and I rubbed my feet on the hook rug as I walked around the side to let Nancy in. Then I looked for a light. There wasn't any electricity but I found a kerosene lantern and some matches by the stove.

Nancy was standing by the card table when the lantern ignited. She crossed her arms, embarrassed at her nakedness now that we were away from the Institute.

"Do you think they have some clothes?" she asked, heading into the small bedroom and pulling a couple of pairs of jeans and some sweatshirts out of a big chest of drawers. They were about a size 56 long and must have been designed for Paul Bunyan. We toweled ourselves off and put them on anyway, looking like a pair of refugees from a Laurel and Hardy movie. Outside, the wind was still howling, and Nancy stood making faces in the full-length mirror while I made a fire in the fireplace.

When that was done, she came and sat down opposite me. I took one look at her and jumped up again. "How about something to eat?" I said, finding a can of pork and beans in the cupboard. I held it up for her inspection. "Just the thing for a rainy night when you lose two cars and one person." I opened the can and spooned the contents into a sauce pan. The stove wasn't working, so I carried the can back with me and held it over the fire.

"You know, you look sexier with your clothes on," I said.

"Bullshit!"

"No, no, I mean it. It's true of all women. They all look sexier with their clothes on. Once they're naked, the mystery is gone. You can't wonder what they look like naked anymore. Take the movies for example. Now who's sexier . . . Marlene Dietrich or Linda Lovelace? And you never see Marlene Dietrich naked." I was yakking nonstop. I couldn't shut up.

"I think you're a prude," she said.

"Something like that."

The fire was searing my fingers and I switched hands, leaning the saucepan against the brick.

"What do you think that guy wanted with those photographs?" she asked.

"He was going to sell them to a French postcard company. Look, let's not talk about it now. The whole thing gives me a headache."

I looked at her. The light from the fire was turning her hair a brilliant red.

"Should we sleep together now?" she asked.

"Yeah . . . probably."

"What do you mean, probably?"

"Well, I'm not sure whether it's blind passion or relief from not flying over a cliff in a mudslide."

"What difference does it make?"

"I don't know."

She took the spoon from me and began to stir the beans. "Suppose I were to tell you that I hadn't slept with anybody since I met Jock."

"I'd be surprised."

"Why?"

"You had an open marriage."

"That doesn't mean anything. You could live your whole life never having sex with anyone but your husband and still have an open marriage. Or you could make love with everyone you know and be totally unliberated."

"Then what's the point of having it?"

"It's just freedom from the constraint of monogamy. That's all."

"You sound like Cynthia Hardwick."

"Or Jock." She laughed, propping the saucepan on a log

and leaning against the brick. "How'd you ever become a private detective anyway?"

"You really want to know?"

"Uh huh."

"Well, I'd just dropped out of law school and was flat broke in San Francisco and this lawyer friend of mine needed somebody to help prove a cop beat up this peace demonstrator at Santa Rita. So I did it and one thing led to another and . . ."

"Here you are."

"Yeah, here I am."

The flames were shooting high off the logs now, licking the sides of the saucepan, turning it black. We stared at the fire and then at each other.

"So how many men have there been in your life?"

"Seven. Jock was the last."

She rolled over and stretched out on the rug. I slid down next to her, our bodies about six inches apart.

"Still attracted by the myth of the virgin?"

"Sure. I can show you what it's really like . . . or fall flat on my face."

"And that's erotic?"

"Maybe more than that."

I reached out and touched her hair. At the bottom, it was still damp from the rain.

"This is going to have to be slow," she said. And she ran the tips of her fingers across my face, caressing my lips, running her wrist around my neck. I took her by the arms and drew her toward me, sensing her body, pressing my thighs against hers. Her breasts pushed against my shirt. We kissed a little with our lips shut. I slid my hand under her sweatshirt. She sighed and breathed heavily. I felt myself getting hard.

"Wait!" she shouted, pulling away.

"What's wrong?"

"The beans. They're burning!"

She was right. They were boiling over the side and smoking fiercely. I jumped up and raced around the kitchen, looking for something to pull them out with. I found a barbecue fork in the drawer and knocked them off the log onto the brick in front of the fireplace.

Then I looked at Nancy. She was smiling up at me, unzipping the fly of her baggy pants. I knelt down on top of her, unsnapping the buttons and pulling off my jeans. She wiggled out of her clothes, sliding beneath me. I gladly kissed off the hundred a day plus expenses. I could still smell the mud and rain in her hair as we made love. It never smelled so good.

13

The next morning, the sun was shining and the birds were singing. The horses were whinnying in the stable and a balmy breeze was blowing through an open window. I was lying next to a beautiful woman and I was filled with anxiety. Sweating. It was eight o'clock. In about nine hours the Cubans would be moving in on my kids.

I sat up and looked at Nancy. She was sleeping with her head on the carpet and her feet propped on the seat of a bentwood rocker. Her face was cocked to the side and she had a beatific smile on her lips. I hated to wake her.

"Do you know how to ride a horse?" I asked.

She stirred slightly and groaned, turning her eyes away from the sun.

"Do you know how to ride a horse?"

"What?"

"I said —"

"You asked — do I know how to ride?"

"Right. Do you?"

"Sure. Jock and I went every Thursday morning in Central Park."

"Let's see if we can find a horse. Otherwise we'll have to walk."

She sat up and stared at me. "Jesus, you like to get up

91

early, don't you?"

"We're running out of time. I've got to get my kids out of hock."

I grabbed her arm and pulled her up. "Don't push. I'm with you."

"I'll remember that," I said and kissed her on the lips.

I went into the bathroom and splashed some water on my face. Then I went back into the living room and wrote a thank-you note to the owner of the ranch, attaching a twenty dollar bill to pay for the window, etc.

Nancy followed me into the bathroom. "I don't know why you're hurrying so much. You already know that it's Greenglass."

"Maybe . . . But I've still got to get ahold of the tapes."

I waited for Nancy to wash up; then we started down the road toward Topanga Center. No horses in sight, so we hiked. Along the way we could see evidence of other slides, some fences knocked down and a house with a pile of mud three feet high on the front porch. I looked around for a sign of the dead man or the two cars, but I couldn't find them. I did see the old Jag in the ditch by the river, untouched by the natural disaster though its tires were still flat. I tapped the hood for luck as we passed on.

At the top of Tuna, we caught a ride down to the shopping center with a construction worker in a Datsun pick-up. He was full of talk about the mudslide. Biggest one they'd had in years, he said. Twenty, thirty cars lost, not to mention houses. The slides were scarier than the fires, if you asked him. They happened so suddenly. You didn't have time to get out. That way they were more like quakes, but with a warning from the weather of course. Next time we'd know better than to slip around a roadblock. After all, you can't mess around with Mother Nature. He thought that was a big joke, but I knew what he meant.

When we got to the shopping center, Nancy went into a boutique to buy some clothes that fit while I headed into the post office coffee shop to make some phone calls.

92

The first one was to the Disneyland Hotel. Jacob answered the phone.

"Hello, this is your dad."

"Oh . . . hi."

"Remember me?"

"Yeah."

"How are things?"

"Okay."

"Is that all?"

"What?"

"Is that all you have to say?"

"Oh . . . yeah."

"Nothing happened?"

"No . . . Hey, listen, I've got to get off. We're late."

"You're late?"

"The park opens at ten and it's already five after."

Oh, shit, I thought to myself. "Weren't you there all day yesterday?"

"Yeah, but we only got through the Haunted House once and we didn't even get on the Matterhorn. The lines were too long."

"Tough luck. I had a bit of a ride myself."

There was a short silence, then, "Well, good-bye . . ."

"Good-bye." I started to hang up.

"Oh, wait a second."

"What?"

"What's hydroponics?"

"Hydroponics?"

"You know, what Mom wrote about on the postcard that's going to save everybody."

"I think it's something to do with growing plants in the ocean for food."

"Yucch . . . Mom knows I don't like vegetables," he said and hung up.

My next call was to the rent-a-car agency. I figured they'd be mighty pissed losing one of their autos over a cliff so I beat them to the punch with a long harangue about defective brakes and how could they let people go driving around like that in such a high-risk environment. "Would you send a man into the Sahara with a faulty cooling system?" I slammed my fist on the counter of the phone booth.

The manager got on the phone sounding most apologetic and offered to replace the car with any model I wished. "I want it here in twenty minutes!" I said. "And send a compact. I don't want one of those gas guzzlers!"

Then I called the police and told them to look for a dead body twenty feet under the mud near the old ranch off Tuna Canyon. I hung up in a hurry before they could trace it.

And then I bit my lip and made the most important call.

"Chateau Marmont. Grace speaking. How are you today?"

"I'm all right. How are you?"

"Hey . . . do I know you?"

"I don't know. Do you?"

"Your voice sounds familiar. Do you know a guy named Henry who has a lot of parties out at Marina del Rey?"

"No."

"Come on. The one with the catamaran on Panay Way. I know I met you there."

"No, you didn't."

"Yes, I did. I've got it now. Your name is Charlie Petrakis and you're a bouzouki player at the Athenian."

"Wrong. My name is Moses Wine and I called to see if there were any messages for me. They'd be in the Nancy Hecht box, bungalow five."

"Okay, okay . . . Hey," she whistled into the phone, "you a gangster or something?"

"Why?"

"You got a message from Meyer Greenglass."

"What does it say?"

"'Dear Mr. Wine: Read yesterday's *Variety*, page four, column six.'"

"What?"

"That's what it says, yesterday's *Variety*, page —"

"I heard you," I said. "Thanks."

94

I hung up and stumbled out of the phone booth into the coffee shop. The same crew from two days ago was still sitting there, discussing a poem by Charles Olson. One of them had read it, but I couldn't figure out which.

"What's up?" Nancy asked, coming in the door wearing a white nightgown dress that looked like thrift shop *shmate*.

"He's sending us on a treasure hunt and this is the first clue. Read *Variety*, page four, column six . . . You look real classy. Haight-Ashbury 1967."

"It was this or a macramé bikini."

We went outside and waited for the car. It was there right on schedule, a Vega hatchback that pulled up rattling like a subway car.

"Sign here, please," said a polite young man, jumping out and handing me the forms to sign. "You can drop me back in Woodland Hills."

"We'll have to check it out first."

"What?"

I bent over and inspected the car. "You know, check it out to be sure it's running all right. The front end looks like it needs aligning."

"Oh?"

I unlocked the door for Nancy and got in behind the wheel. "Step back," I called out to him.

"What?"

"Back up and walk around the other side of the store to where I can't see you." He looked baffled. "Then I can drive around the building and you can check the front end coming through."

"Oh, okay."

He waved to me and walked off through the alley to the back of the store. When he was out of sight, I sped off down Topanga Boulevard to the ocean. I hated to do it to the guy, but I didn't have enough time to sidetrack all the way over to Woodland Hills.

Variety, yesterday's *Variety*, I thought as we drew nearer the Pacific. I turned left on the Coast Highway, then left again on the ramp leading up to Santa Monica. Driving along Wilshire, I made a right on Sixth Street and headed straight for the public library. I got out and pushed through the doors, going directly to the reference desk. The librarian gave me an arrogant look when I requested the show business periodical. I almost felt like telling her I wasn't an out-of-work actor, that I was something legitimate like a private dick. I took the newspaper instead and flipped to page four, running my finger along to the sixth column.

BIG COOLER FREEZES PRODUCTION

Fox execs nixed production Monday on producer Sal Gruskow's *The Badass Brigade* due to a malfunction in the air conditioning on Stage Nine.

Star Dakota Dawn refused to continue her love scene in temperatures of 115 degrees. "It threw my concentration," she said.

Production resumes today on Stage Four. Stage Nine will remain out of use indefinitely due to problems of union jurisdiction.

So Greenglass wanted me to know Gruskow's air conditioning had a malfunction. I folded the paper and returned it to the librarian.

I kissed Nancy again as I got back in the car and we headed for Fox. On the way over we listened to the news. Dichter's clean-up campaign was going full force. In the last two days they had closed down twelve massage parlors, five bookstores and a trio of movie theaters on the Strip. At the rate he was going, by next week you wouldn't be able to get an alcohol rub for a backache.

We had more trouble getting on the lot this time. Gruskow hadn't left my name with the guard, but his secretary remembered who I was and persuaded him to let us pass. But when we got to Gruskow's office, he wasn't there and the secretary had disappeared. Matt Zimmerman was pacing around in the corridor looking very upset.

"I don't know what to do," said the young screenwriter,

pointing inside at Lars Gundersen, who was staring moodily out the office window. "Sal leaves us here to hammer out the gangster story, really get it set, and he won't talk to me. All he wants to do is meditate and listen to Sibelius."

"He's probably homesick."

"Maybe so, but Sal's going to have my ass. My option comes up in two days."

"Where is Sal anyway?"

"Anywhere and everywhere. Try Stage Four."

Gruskow wasn't on Stage Four. After that we tried the commissary and the cutting room, where another of his films was in production. Nobody knew where to find him. I was about to give up when I saw him getting into his Mercedes with a black actress I took to be Dakota Dawn.

"Well, well, Moses Wine." He insisted on shaking my hand. "How's the investigation going? Find out if Hecht really committed suicide?"

"Nothing for sure."

"This business, I wouldn't wish it on a dog." He glanced over at Nancy, removing some dust from the hood of his Mercedes with his fingers.

"I heard you had some trouble on Stage Nine the other day."

"Trouble? It was a shitstorm! Poor Dakota here almost died of heat prostration." He put his arm around the actress, pushing his hand through her shoulder strap made of linked gold chain.

"Which stage is number nine?" I asked.

He pointed down the end of the Western street to a blue building with its corner sticking out from behind the saloon.

"Can we go there?"

"The place is shut down until the fucking union decides who has jurisdiction to fix the air conditioning."

"Let's go anyway."

"It's important?"

I nodded.

"Okay, but we gotta be quick. Dakota and I have a one

o'clock reservation at Mr. Chow's."

Nancy and I followed him over to the hangar-sized stage and entered through a crack between the large sliding doors. The place was dark and cavernous. "Can you get the lights?" I asked Gruskow, and he flicked on some work lights around the side. I stared up at the four-foot-square aluminum air-conditioning ducts hung about ten feet below the ceiling, a steel ladder and an elevator platform running up the wall to them. I walked over and looked up the ladder, then started to climb.

"You ever find Meiko?" Gruskow called out as I neared the top, stopping at the edge of the elevator platform. The duct tilted down in front of me; a mesh grating was attached to the end with a flange. "Bitch!" he continued. "Ruining two days of photography at twenty thousand a shot. That's the last time she works in this town!"

I leaned forward and grabbed the flange, twisting it upwards and removing the grate. Jiggling the frame, I heard a strange grinding noise, then a sudden whoosh. I moved just in time to avoid the trajectory of a dead yellow lady, who came flying out of the duct like a cannonball.

Holding my breath, I grabbed the ladder tightly and started climbing down again. I could see the woman's once-beautiful limbs splayed out on the floor of the sound stage beneath me. Her skull was crushed and her face was twisted around like an owl's. A number of tiny brown dots ran up and down the small of her back as if she had been tortured with a burning cigarette. It was a horrible sight.

14

"How did Greenglass know Meiko was there?" she repeated.

"I don't know."

"He must have killed her, or had her killed."

"And leave his name with the location of the body signed on the message desk at the Chateau Marmont? He's more sophisticated than that."

"Then what was he doing?"

"Giving us a sign . . . showing us he wasn't guilty."

Nancy looked at me in confusion. It was already twelve thirty and we were driving along Sunset, headed east. I was worried about the time. It had taken the better part of thirty minutes convincing Gruskow to let us off the lot.

"Okay," said Nancy. "Explain to me how that shows he isn't guilty."

"Try this — First of all, Meyer's proven Jock did have an alibi and that Meiko was killed most likely by somebody who wanted to see Jock take the rap for Debbie Frank's murder . . . Right?"

Nancy nodded.

"Therefore, probability two, you were right all the time. Jock was murdered, using Deborah Frank's killing as a convenient scapegoat, and the suicide note was a phony."

"Okay," she said, her voice weakening. "I follow that."

"Now for the subtle part — the little Talmudic fillip from the Jewish gangster. If Greenglass knew that Jock's alibi was good, then he also knew Jock didn't kill Deborah. Therefore, he, Greenglass, would have no reason to kill Jock and no niece's murder to avenge."

"So the motive we imputed to Greenglass is false."

"That's right. He's innocent. He didn't want to revenge himself on Jock because he already knew Jock wasn't guilty. As simple as that."

"Then where are we?" she asked.

I felt myself sink as the truth made itself depressingly clear. "Nowhere," I said.

"What're you going to do?"

"There's only one thing left."

"What?"

"Go see the Cubans. Tell them I haven't got the tapes but try to convince them to lay off the kids anyway . . . I don't have any choice." I turned into the driveway behind the Marmont, parking at the end of the path to the bungalows. I leaned over Nancy and opened the door. She didn't move, smiling sardonically.

"That's man's work, huh?"

I sat up straight, leaving the door open, and stared at her. "It's not man's work or woman's work. Those motherfuckers are killers. Now you can stay or you can come. Do what you want. Just do it quickly."

She thought about it for a moment, then slid her hand along the seat until she reached my thigh. "What do you want me to do?" she asked.

"Oh, well . . ."

"Are you going to fall in love with me?"

"What does that have to do with it?"

"I don't know. Nothing, I guess . . . Kiss me good-bye."

I leaned over and kissed her. I had meant to make it short, but the kiss started to lengthen, deepen, bringing back the passion of the previous night. Nancy was the first to break away.

"I don't think you should," she said.

"What?"

"Fall in love with me."

"Why not?"

"You wouldn't understand."

"What makes you think I am?"

"It's that look in your eye. I've seen it before. In the movies."

"You believe in that romantic crap?"

"No. But you might."

I looked at her, wondering. "See you tonight," I said and drove off onto Sunset.

The Cubans lived on my turf, Echo Park. They were a small group, but growing, filtering in from Miami in tens and twenties, catching the overflow from Little Havana. In the late sixties there were only a few Cuban restaurants and grocery stores. Now there were clothiers, realtors, doctors, dentists, print shops, newspapers, a parochial school and several night clubs where you could dance the *pachanga* and listen to the music of the *bandas tropicales*. Yet they remained a close-knit community despite their size, some of them still living on the illusion of returning to the island and a lot more paying it lip service.

The first place I tried to find Santiago Martin was the Batey Market, a grocery store on the corner of Sunset and Silver Lake Boulevard. I often bought coffee there and I knew the manager, an old black man from Oriente Province who came to the States during the Batista period, long before Castro.

"How're you doin', Carlos?"

"*Hola, amigo,*" he said, reaching for a tin of Café Gavina and a box of filter papers. He could never remember my name, but he knew what I wanted.

I shook my head. "Next week . . . Today I'm looking for something else, a big Cuban operator named Santiago Martin. You know him?"

"Personally, no. He doesn't come into this market. And I doubt he does his own shopping anyway."

"You know where I can find him?"

"Try the offices of the newspaper *20 de Mayo*. Under the freeway bridge by Echo Park Lake."

The offices were closed. I looked inside. The newspaper was a bi-weekly and wouldn't be open until Thursday. Through the window I could see a large photograph of Havana and a blow-up of Castro that had been used as a dart board. Above that was a portrait of Alfredo Zayas, President of Cuba from 1921-1925. Each of these exiled groups had its own peculiar ideology, its own heroes.

I walked along Sunset, looking into the bakeries and record stores, wondering which were Cuban and which Mexican, getting more apprehensive by the moment. I was baffled and behaving erratically. The situation with the kids was getting to me. I had to keep my head.

Then I remembered the obvious and went into a phone booth to look up the number of Viajes Miami. I dialed it and was given a referral number in the 628 area, Echo Park. I dialed again.

"Maugey Development Company."

"I'd like to speak with Santiago Martin."

"Mr. Martin is at lunch."

"Do you know where he is?"

"I'm sorry, but I'm not allowed to disclose that information."

"But this is an emergency. I'm Mr. Brownlow, Mr. Martin's new tax consultant. There's a discrepancy on his quarterly returns which must be adjusted immediately to avoid an audit!"

"Can't it wait for later this afternoon?"

"By that time the IRS in Washington will be closed!"

She put me on hold. I held my breath, counting the seconds. It was a long shot. In a minute and a half she was back on the line.

102

"He's at La Guantanamera on Temple Street."

"Thanks."

La Guantanamera was five minutes away, a Cuban restaurant and night club on the corner of Westmoreland next to an insurance agency and a record store. At night, it featured a vocal group, Chocolate y Sylvia, but now it was silent as I entered, the front room dark except for a green light over the bar. I passed through to the dining room, a larger area with a skylight and potted palms. The walls were decorated with pastoral oil paintings of the Cuban countryside, black men stripped to the waist like Winslow Homer's "Gulf Stream," their glistening machetes poised over clumps of sugar cane.

The dining room was empty with the exception of Martin's party. He sat, surrounded by his gunsels, at a round table in the corner, eating a large portion of fish stew with fried bananas. He stood up as I approached him, extending his hand.

"Mr. Wine. So good to see you. My secretary informed me you were on your way."

"Your — ?"

He pointed at a telephone on the table. "You needn't have gone to such lengths. I left my card on your dining room table . . . Now, where are the tapes?"

"That's the problem, Mr. Martin. Locating the tapes hasn't been so easy."

"Why?"

"I don't know what's on them, for one thing. And I don't know who has them, for another."

He smiled, breaking open the claw of a crab. "Come on, Mr. Wine. Take a guess."

"I would guess they contain incriminating evidence linking the directors of the Sexual Liberation League with someone who might be embarrassed."

"Very good, Mr. Wine. Quite accurate . . . And you expect me to believe you don't know who this someone is?"

"That's right . . ."

"You would just like me to tell you everything I know. What do you think I am, a fool? . . . Sit down."

One of the gunsels pulled up a chair and I sat down across from him.

"What would you like to eat? The *zarzuela* is good. The *media noche* if you are not so hungry."

"I don't feel like eating, Mr. Martin."

"Ah, you are concerned about your children. How are they enjoying Disneyland? I try to visit there twice a year myself . . . I have six children, you know." He stared at me for a moment, then pulled out his wallet, withdrawing a Polaroid snapshot of six beaming kids at an alligator farm. "Back in Miami," he said. "See. That's Jorge, the oldest. And Esteban . . . We are both lucky to have sons, Mr. Wine."

"I like girls too, Mr. Martin."

"Ah, well, naturally," he said, snapping his fingers for the waiter. "*Manuel, más plátanos. Y una cerveza.*" He turned to me. "You don't mind? . . . I'm still hungry."

I leaned in toward him while he ate. "Look, I think you've made a mistake about me. I have some new evidence that should change your mind about things."

"You do?"

"Hecht didn't commit suicide."

"Oh."

"Meiko, the Japanese girl who was his alibi, was found stiffed in an air-conditioning duct at the Twentieth Century Fox studio."

"Stiffed?"

"*Asesinato.*"

"Ah . . ." Santiago smiled, attacking his second helping of fried bananas. "They all come to that end, those girls. All they want is money. They are too greedy."

"Greedy? Her back was covered with cigarette burns, Señor Martin."

"Oh. A pity." His eyes flickered with recognition. He must have known her at the Phrontistery. He managed the place, after all. "And what is this all supposed to prove?" he asked.

104

"That Hecht was murdered."

"Ah."

"And probably by the same person who murdered Deborah Frank."

"Oh."

"And whoever murdered him took the tapes."

"Indeed . . . And what difference does that make?"

"What difference? You find the murderer and you find the tapes!"

He threw up his hands. "But, of course! And you did it. You are working for El Jefe and you murdered him!"

"Do I look like a murderer?"

"That's not important. Either you did it or El Jefe did it himself and you helped him. That does not matter. What matters is the tapes . . . And, of course, your children. I understand they have liked well the Haunted House. They have visited it twice."

"Lay off those kids, Martin." Bastard. I was starting to sweat. "I'll call the police."

"The police?" He laughed. "Why don't you call El Jefe?"

This El Jefe business was confusing me. Whoever he was, Martin wasn't ready to believe I didn't work for him. I had to shift gears.

"Suppose El Jefe doesn't have the tapes? Suppose they're in the hands of a third party who's out to get him?"

Martin stopped and looked at me, a forkful of banana halfway to his mouth. "And who would want to do that?" He brought it up and swallowed it.

"He has enemies."

"That is true." Martin seemed to be listening for the first time.

"He might be willing to make a deal with you."

"Ah, well, I am here."

"Do you have any particular message you would like me to convey to him?"

"Tell him . . . not to betray his old friends."

Suddenly, we were interrupted by a loud, smashing noise.

105

Then a familiar voice: "Listen, fucker, you keep your hands off me or I'll let you have it right in the balls with the broken end of a Wild Turkey."

It was Gunther, pinned back against the bar by two of the gunsels, brandishing a smashed whiskey bottle.

"I'm gonna play tic-tac-toe on your stomachs, birdbrains!" He started to advance on them like a bullfighter moving in for the final kill.

"*Carajo!*" said one of the gunsels, pulling a Browning automatic. Gunther poked at him with the bottle. The gunsel fired, mercifully smashing a cocktail shaker at his feet, sending the glass spraying all over the counter of the bar. But Gunther continued to advance, swiping at him crazily, coming within an inch of his chin with the jagged edge of the bottle.

"*No se puede!*" yelled the other gunsel, ducking low and taking out his pistol. He aimed it carefully at Gunther's head.

"Go ahead and try, shithead!" said Gunther, turning to face him. I had visions of his brains splattered against the mirror.

I jumped up. "He's one of us!" I shouted.

The gunsels wheeled around.

"One of your men?" said Santiago, patting his lips with a paper napkin.

"He works for El Jefe."

"I see."

"I'll take care of him." I walked over and grabbed Gunther by the arm. "Keep moving, shmuck," I whispered to him "and don't look back." We walked past the puzzled gunsels out of the restaurant.

"Found you again," he said, grinning, when we reached the alley.

"Very funny, motherfucker," I said, ramming him against the wall. "This time you nearly blew the case and got my kids killed to boot. Listen, Robin Hood, I admire your style, but I prefer to work alone."

"And just when I've broken the case wide open."

"The only case you ever broke open was Wild Turkey.

And that was when someone else was paying."

"Ho, ho, ho. Your problem is you don't know who your friends are!"

"Who are they?"

"Your humble servant of the Fourth Estate." He smiled and dug into his pocket, extracting a handful of newspaper clippings. "From the basement of the restaurant."

"Let's see them," I said.

He unclenched his fist and I thumbed through the clippings. There were about a half dozen from various papers, all dated from spring 1971 and all concerning the same event — the tenth anniversary of the Bay of Pigs invasion.

"Discontented Cubans. What else is new? You could tell that by looking at the paintings on the wall." I started to hand back the wad of old paper clippings.

"You think so? Take a look at that one."

He pointed to a blurred news photo of eight men standing in front of a swimming pool, their arms linked in comradely bravura. The caption beneath read:

CUBA LIBRE, REGRESAMOS
FREE CUBA, WE SHALL RETURN

Men of the Third Battalion of the ill-fated Bay of Pigs invasion meet with their old Chief.

I studied the faces of the men of the Third Battalion, easily recognizing Santiago Martin and his friends among them. But it was the face of the "Chief" that stunned me. I had to look at him three times to be certain I was correct. But I was. It was Attorney General Frank Dichter.

"So that's El Jefe," I said.

"Seems like, don't it?"

15

"What kind of rolling papers do you use?"

"Rolling papers?"

"You know — Zig-Zag, Bambu. Wheat straw or regular."

"Shit, I don't care. As long as it isn't licorice . . . The cops notice colors when you're driving." I looked over at him as I drove. He had out a pencil and paper and was taking notes.

"What're your feelings about search and seizure laws?"

"You're still doing that goddamn article?"

"You know what Warhol said about everybody in America being famous for ten minutes . . . Well, your time has come!"

He reached into his pocket for a vial of pink and yellow pills, taking one of each. I made a short prayer and turned off Little Santa Monica to Century City. The whole complex had the look of some austere, lunar city, the sun reflecting brilliantly off the sheer glass façades. I took a right at the shopping center and pulled into the parking lot of the Century Plaza Hotel, hopping out fast with Gunther right behind me. It was two thirty-five.

"Do you read Nietzsche?" he asked as we crossed by Yamato's heading for the back door of the hotel.

"No."

"What about Gurdjieff?"

I shook my head.

"Have you ever been in Arica training?"

"No. But the last time I had my Tarot cards read I drew the Juggler."

"I would have figured you for the Hanged Man."

I pushed past him and we entered the lower level of the building, which was lined with overpriced gift shops. I stopped at a florist and bought their cheapest bouquet. It came in a plastic urn shaped like a Greek amphora; the flowers were gladiolas. I filled out a gift card and slipped it inside while the saleswoman wrapped the whole package in green wax paper.

Then we took the escalator to the main lobby, an overly grand salon where elegant fixtures mixed with the worst schlock. The runner carpets were patterned with *fleurs-de-lis*. The doormen were dressed as Beefeaters. I walked past them to the house phones and picked up the first one in line.

"Operator."

"Attorney General Dichter's room, please."

"Lines are busy. Can you hold?"

"No. I'll call back . . . What number is that?"

"904."

"Thanks."

I hung up.

I nodded to Gunther and we rode up in the elevator together, watching the numbers flash above the door to a canned version of "September Song." The elevator paused on the seventh floor and then stopped on the ninth, opening onto a long corridor leading to Dichter's room. Two hulking plainclothesmen were posed in front, blocking the way like a pair of Sherman tanks on loan from El Toro Marine Base.

"Howdy," I said, waltzing past them with a wink and approaching Dichter's door as if it were the most natural thing in the world.

I felt a meaty hand on my shoulder. "Where do you think you're goin'?"

"Flowers for the Attorney General," I said without looking back.

"Flowers? What does the Attorney General want with flowers?"

"I didn't send them, mister."

I turned around and smiled my most disingenuous smile. The plainclothesman looked back and forth between Gunther and me.

"Lemme see that!" He grabbed the bouquet away and started rifling through the stems.

"Careful," I said. "That's *Ficus pumila*. Very fragile."

The plainclothesman gave me a nasty look and reached for the gift card.

"Unh, unh, unh." I wagged my finger at him. "I'm sure that's confidential."

He put the card back and stared at me for a moment. "All right," he said. "But this bimbo stays outside."

Gunther looked disappointed.

I knocked on the door. Dichter was in his shirtsleeves when he answered, carrying the telephone in one hand with his head cocked to the receiver. He motioned me to enter. I shut the door behind me and crossed to the end table, unwrapping the bouquet and prettying it up a bit while listening to snatches of his conversation. He was talking to the press — probably somebody important like a columnist or a commentator — taking him into his confidence and scoring points.

"Keep this under your hat, Al, but tomorrow, at the Women's Luncheon, we'll be making some major announcements. They'll be out of business from one end of the state to the other. Some big heads are going to roll. We're not sparing anybody . . . Now, look, people can say what they want, but this isn't politically motivated. We're two years away from any election."

He reached into his pocket and pulled out a quarter, holding it out for me. I didn't move. He turned to me, puzzled. I handed him the gift card. He opened it and read, still listening to the phone call. His expression didn't change, but I had a sense of his inner reaction as he studied the words I wrote:

"Greetings from beyond the grave — Jock Hecht."

He stuffed the card back in its envelope and stuck it in his pocket. "Okay, Al, I'll be calling you again . . ."

He hung up.

"What's this about?"

"You know what it's about."

"No, I don't. But I know Jock Hecht committed suicide two days ago."

"Let's not fool around, Dichter. I don't have time for that. Where are the tapes?"

"Tapes?"

"You know what I mean. Now do you want me to call Al or some other columnist and tell him you murdered Jock Hecht — or are you going to surrender?"

"What *are* you talking about?"

"Come on, Dichter! It's all there. First you murdered Deborah Frank and then Jock Hecht. Not to mention Meiko to keep it all under wraps."

"What on earth for?"

"Because they were going to expose your link to a group of Cubans who run the Sexual Liberation League. It's all there on the tapes.

"Oh, my, my," he started to laugh.

"Do you deny knowing Santiago Martin?"

"Santiago Martin?" He hesitated a moment, making a show of searching his memory. "Santiago Martin? . . . Oh, yes . . . an intense man with a mustache."

"You were his Chief."

"Not his Chief. His Adviser."

"So you don't deny you were involved in the Bay of Pigs?"

"Of course not. It's all in the history books. I helped train the freedom fighters in Florida and later in Guatemala."

"Freedom fighters? Gangsters is more like it!" This guy was hard to take.

"I'm proud of having served my country." Dichter gave me a sardonic look. "Is that all you have, that I knew these people thirteen years ago?"

"You saw them again in '71."

"On the tenth anniversary of the invasion. For a reunion. What does that prove? . . . And now, if you will excuse me, I am very busy."

"I'm not leaving without the tapes, Dichter."

"You're not leaving?"

"You're a murderer, Dichter! Those bastards are threatening my kids."

"A murderer? Don't be ridiculous! How did I commit these murders? With my own two hands?"

"That makes sense to me. It would have taken somebody powerful and respected to enter Hecht's bungalow and set up a suicide like that. There was no evidence of a struggle."

He was still smiling. "And when were these murders committed?"

"Deborah Frank was killed three nights ago, Jock Hecht the following evening."

"Three nights ago I was having dinner with the Governor in Sacramento. The following night I was sitting in this room with my wife."

"Having dinner with the Governor? You expect me to believe that?"

"Get out of here before I have you arrested for breaking and entering."

"Give me the tapes, Dichter. You're lying."

"Lying? I am the Attorney General of this state and you —"

"Give me the tapes!"

"Tapes? You gotta be joking? If those tapes contained what you said, they would have been instantly erased." He hesitated and looked at me. "Now I recognize you. You're the wise-guy Jewish detective from the press conference!" He reached for the phone and pushed the intercom. "Gibson! Gibson!"

He glared at me. It took me about half a second to realize what was up. Then I bolted from the room, slamming the door behind me, and ran past the plainclothesman as he reached for the phone.

"Come on," I said, grabbing Gunther on the way and pulling him toward the elevator. I could hear the men start out after us before I could press the button. Seconds passed and the two cops rounded the corner. I whipped around, catching one of them in the stomach, and headed down the other corridor. Gunther was right on my heels, moving fast.

We reached the service exit at the other end and raced down the steps like two whirling dervishes. By the time we were on the eighth floor, an alarm bell was ringing. By the seventh, we heard men's voices in the corridor.

"Get 'em on the sixth," someone shouted.

I froze and nodded to Gunther. We slowly climbed back up the stairs to the eighth floor and crept out into the hall. A group of conventioneers was walking toward us, headed for the elevator. They wore fezlike caps and appeared a little tipsy.

"You fellas with the AAMPDA?" one of them asked.

"You got it," I said, falling in behind them. "What you guys got for tonight? A little nooky?"

"Bet your sweet ass!"

"Mind if we tag along?"

"Why the hell not?"

We all arrived at the elevator, nodding and smiling.

"Where 'bouts you fellas from?" one asked me.

"Butte. Butte, Montana."

"Mighty fine country around there."

"I'll say."

"You know Mort Higginson?"

"Sure do."

"How is old Mort?"

"Oh, the same."

"He damn well should be," said another of them. "He's been dead since fall '68."

We were spared having to rectify this discrepancy by the arrival of the elevator. Gunther and I took a quick look at each other, smiled feebly and started through the open door. But we were met halfway by two plainclothesmen standing

113

with their arms folded.

"It's the creeps!" said Gunther, delivering a swift kick in the gut to the fatter of the two.

We turned on our heels and made tracks back to the service stairs. Only this time we could hear people coming up from below. And down from above.

"Now what?" he said.

"We split up." I pointed down the stairs. "Meet me at the car in ten minutes!"

He gave me a last look, crossed his motorcycle jacket and barreled down the stairs at a breakneck clip. *"Mon semblable, mon frère!"* I heard him cry.

I backed up one step at a time, listening for the voices over my head. When they stopped, I ran up to the ninth floor, three steps at a time. The corridor in front of Dichter's room was empty. I entered and lingered by his door a second, catching some final pearls of wisdom. He was on the phone again, resuming his conversation. "I'll tell you, Al . . . a man in my position. I am subject to a lot of false accusations. You wouldn't believe some of them. Even you press boys would be embarrassed to print them."

I crept past to the elevator. I pushed the button, hoping they wouldn't suspect I was still on the ninth floor and that it would be empty when it reached me. It started up. I checked my watch. Ten minutes to four. That gave me an hour and ten minutes to get to Disneyland at the peak of rush hour.

The elevator arrived. When it opened, a couple of bellboys got out, talking to each other. I stepped inside and pressed number one. We descended quickly, spurred on by an uptempo version of "Autumn Leaves" from the Musak.

The lobby was suspiciously quiet when the car reached the bottom. No policemen. No security guards. Not even any Beefeaters. I walked out to the center and headed for a revolving door, feeling vaguely uneasy. Then I heard a loud scream. I turned to see Gunther running up the down escalator, about two steps ahead of a dozen uniformed police and plainclothesmen. He reached the top, looked both ways and darted across the lobby toward the back. The posse formed a phalanx and advanced, forcing him toward the wall. He backed against the glass. They were about to pounce when he yelled, "Cazart!" and jumped over the sofa, smashing through the picture window onto the marble floor of a sunken patio.

I hung back at the edge of the crowd swarming toward him. Looking down, I could see him hopping about like a madman, grabbing his leg and cursing as the police encircled him.

I slipped out a side exit.

16

The Santa Ana Freeway between Los Angeles and Anaheim is the missing tenth ring of Dante's Inferno — fifty miles of franchise food stands, used-car lots, discount furniture outlets, oil refineries, rubber factories and trailer parks — the kind of environment that would kill a prairie dog just to look at it.

That afternoon I got it all in slow motion. The traffic was moving like corpuscles through a cholesterol-rotted artery. First came the grimy ramparts of Boyle Heights, then the badlands of Pico Rivera and the City of Commerce, antiseptic think tanks mixed with industrial power plants and cheap-jack motels. Then came the Orange County border with its pseudo-dairies and vanishing citrus groves, the rancid air smelling of ozone and Nixon.

I pushed on, the traffic barely moving, the car inching forward at idle without the slightest touch on the accelerator. I took another furtive look at my watch. It was already five, the zero hour, and I was still fifteen miles away. I didn't want to believe Martin would do anything so vicious as take the kids; I didn't want to believe it, but I knew that he could. It wasn't that I didn't have any faith left in human nature. I still had some left, somewhere. It was just that the last decade of American life had reduced it to the size of a desiccated pea.

I flicked on the radio, then flicked it off again. I wasn't in the mood for music and the news only mirrored the atmosphere. Outside, I was passing by the Japanese Village in Buena Park at five miles per hour, its perimeter so "freeway close" you thought you were sloshing through the middle of its exhibition pool like an amphibian with a kimono-clad geisha licking cotton candy and prodding you through the hoop with the dolphins. I could almost hear her inane patter through the car window.

Then the traffic began to break up. I depressed the pedal and accelerated. But as my speed increased, so did my paranoia. I started to see visions, nightmare images of my children in jeopardy, tears streaming down their little faces as they were chased around a ferris wheel by a Cuban gangster with a crowbar in one hand and a German luger in the other. It was as if I had been in a horrible mood and smoked five joints of the meanest marijuana — Thai stick, maybe, or Columbian — letting it take me where it wanted to go, down all the wrong alleys and through all the wrong doors.

. I shook myself to snap out of it, but I only drove faster, weaving dangerously, passing people on the apron with half an eye cocked on the rear-view mirror. I was convinced they were in trouble now. Terrified. Hating myself for leaving them even for a minute. This was my great failure. My disgrace. When the book of life was written, this would blacken my name forever.

Then I saw the Matterhorn looming ahead, its snowcapped masonite jutting over concrete abutments. The Magic Kingdom was at hand. I veered off the freeway into the parking lot, following the attendants to a spot far to the back of a sea of cars. I jumped out two hundred yards from the entrance, trying to decide whether to wait for the tram or run all the way to the kiosk. I debated for a second, then started running, passing a stalled tram at area "P" and continuing straight on to the ticket booth. I paid for a ticket and walked inside, trying to restrain myself from going off in every direction, trying to stay cool. I headed down the Old Main Street, gazing left and right at the shops and arcades, looking for Sonya and the kids. A life-sized Mickey Mouse passed me by, followed by a Pluto. In the distance I could hear the tinkly sound of "When You Wish Upon a Star." Usually it melted my heart, made me feel like a child again, but tonight it sounded like anxiety music, like "Night on Bald Mountain," that frightening bat monster in Disney's own *Fantasia* rising out of the volcano.

The lights went on, a miasma of yellows, pinks and green. I continued on the circular plaza separating the four amusement zones — Frontierland, Adventureland, Fantasyland, Tomorrowland — gazing back and forth, wondering which one they'd be in. It wasn't crowded that evening, but the park was so vast, so many rides, I couldn't decide. Jacob liked Adventureland but Simon, I knew, preferred Fantasyland. I froze in the center, feeling ineffectual and weakkneed, having visions of incontinence.

Then I saw someone out of the corner of my eye, a dark figure striding toward the gate of Tomorrowland. I wheeled around and ran after him, grabbing him by the forearm and spinning him toward me.

"Hey! . . . Something wrong, mister?"

He wore a Disneyland uniform and a shiny badge.

"No, no. My mistake."

I backed away into the center of the rotunda again. Behind me, a man in a straw hat with a monkey on his shoulder was playing a hurdy-gurdy and selling popcorn.

"Looking for someone?" he asked.

"Yeah."

"You should page 'em. At the front." He pointed toward the information booth.

"Thanks."

I went over and spoke carefully to the clerk. "Sonya Lieberman or Jacob Wine," I said politely. But there was something about using Jewish names in Disneyland that added to my unease. At a moment like this, I didn't want to appear an alien in Orange County. I wanted to be a Phillips

118

or a Johnson or a Jones. Even a Haldeman or an Ehrlichman would have been acceptable. Anything to see my kids again.

The words boomed over the loudspeaker: "Sonya Lieberman or Jacob Wine, pah-lease report to the information booth."

I winced and waited ten minutes. The clerk watched me pace the room, taking larger and larger steps until I was crossing from one wall to the other in two strides, slapping my fist on his desk and touching a portrait of Donald Duck as I went. No one came.

"What's wrong with this thing?" I motioned to his microphone. "Doesn't it reach all over?"

"Sure. Except inside the rides."

"Could they be on any of the rides for this long?"

"Sure . . ."

"Which ones?"

"The Haunted House, the Submarine, Pirates of the Caribbean."

I ran out of the booth. They had been at the Haunted House yesterday. Sonya wouldn't go in the submarine. Tonight they might be on the Pirate Ride. I headed through the gate of Adventureland, past the Tiki Village, the shooting galleries and the tree house à la Swiss Family Robinson to the mock wrought-iron balustrades of the French Quarter. At the end of the street, I could see the lines for the Pirates of the Caribbean. They were mercifully short.

I ripped out a ticket and stood behind a group of teenagers, watching the line weave through the pipe barrier to the gate. A family in front got onto one of the long boats and were whisked off, disappearing down the chute. I jumped onto the next one, pushing my way up to the bow, feeling the whoosh as the cable was released and the flat boat descended the ramp, gliding into the pirates' domain.

I strained my eyes to look ahead, trying to make sense of the black space. But I could see nothing and hear nothing except the gentle lapping of the water against the hull. Did he already have them? Was he out there, sitting beside them, the pistol dug deep into Sonya's ribs? Were they bound and gagged somewhere behind the animated scenery? That sonofabitch!

I grew rigid, gripping the gunnels, watching intently as we rounded a corner. There were fireflies on electric wires dancing in the air before us, the faint sound of a pirate's chant: "Yo, ho, ho, and a bottle of rum!" Then it all opened — cannon, forts, galleons, the sacking of New Orleans. I stood up on the bow and looked over the other boats. There were a half dozen of them in the room, proceeding in a line to the edge of the burning port. Then I saw them. They were in the first boat, heading out of sight. Sonya, Jacob and Simon in front; the Cuban with the hairlip not three seats behind them.

I jumped out of the boat, slipping in the water which surprisingly only came up to my knees, holding onto the wall while I stumbled toward them. People around me started to scream as I leapt out of the water onto the back of the boat, grabbing the Cuban and throwing him off behind the scenery. He tried to run, but I got a vertebra-crushing grip around his neck and pinned him to the raw concrete behind a bare-breasted mermaid.

"You motherfucker! You dirty motherfucker!"

I pummeled him with a force I didn't know I had, kicking him in the groin and smashing his nose in with the back of my fist. He collapsed on the wet cement, trying to slip away. But I was on him in an instant, bashing his head against the floor. I was out of control. His face was raw, blood pouring from his nose and mouth, teeth rattling around in his jaw.

"I'll kill you! I'll kill you!" I shouted, holding him by the ears and shaking him until he nearly passed out.

"No . . . no . . . please . . ." he moaned.

And I would have killed him too. But I stared into his bleary eyes and something snapped inside of me. The fury disappeared. My children were safe and he suddenly seemed so banal, like so much human rubbish.

I went back and hugged the kids.

17

"Would you believe I was a dentist?"

"A what?"

"Back in Havana. I was a dentist. With a good practice. I lived in the Miramar district with my wife."

The Cuban was just coming to. It was eight o'clock at night and we were driving into Los Angeles, Simon asleep on Sonya's lap in the back seat.

"I'd believe it," I said.

Who the fuck wouldn't? I took a look at the poor *shlub*. His name was Felix Ribera and he lived on Vendome Street. I knew that much from his wallet. In the light of the passing cars, he looked like he had been dropped face down from the top of the Occidental Building, then run through the centrifuge at Cal Tech. I had never pulverized anyone so thoroughly before. I hoped I never would again.

"Would you believe they wouldn't let her out?" he continued, half mumbling and peeling the caked blood from his lips. "They wouldn't let my wife out. Goddamn Fidelistas. I leave and they promise to let her out in six months. But she never comes. She says she likes it there ... They brainwashed her, goddamn Fidelistas."

"You sure she was brainwashed?" asked Sonya, getting hot under the collar.

"Sure? Of cour—"

"Maybe she met a nice young revolutionary," Sonya went on.

"Where's Santiago?" I interrupted. This was no time for political arguments.

"Huh?"

"Where's Santiago Martin? Remember him?"

"Oh, yeah . . . At the Club Continental. But don't take me there like this. Please. I'll be in bad trouble. At least let me clean up . . ."

The Club Continental. I knew the place, a big Cuban dance hall on Sunset. I drove home first to drop off Sonya and the kids before heading over. Ribera whimpered and tried to wash his face while I hugged and kissed the boys for a long time, reluctant to leave. They still weren't sure why I had gotten so upset; to them, I guess, it seemed like nothing much had happened. But Jacob was really glad to see me and helped put Simon to bed. On the way out, I made sure Sonya double-locked the door behind me.

Ten minutes later, I was climbing the stairs of the Club Continental, dragging Ribera after me like the carcass of a dead animal. Santiago was at the bar with his cronies, drinking cocktails and making jokes with the waitresses. He didn't bat an eyelash when I held Ribera's head six inches from his face.

"Oh, at last, Mr. Wine. You have brought the tapes."

"Does this look like a tape, Santiago?"

"They are in your pocket."

"There aren't any tapes, Santiago. Your Jefe destroyed them. He told me himself."

"He —?"

"Frank Dichter, your Jefe, destroyed the tapes. He also murdered Jock Hecht and Deborah Frank, probably with his own hands, and I'm personally going to pin it on him." I slammed Ribera's semi-limp body against the top of the bar. Poor bastard. "And if you still think I'm working for him, they should ship you off to a recycling center and send your brains through with the aluminum cans."

He stared at me, confusion showing through his usually cocky visage. In the background, a couple of dancers slid across the floor, the timbale player laying down a sharp meringue beat behind them.

I started for the stairs. "See you around, Santiago." He didn't say anything. "And keep your *gusano* creeps away from my children. Since I'm not working for the Attorney General, I'd be delighted to report you for kidnapping!"

I slammed the door of the dance hall and headed for the car, driving over to the Marmont to see Nancy. Traffic had thinned out now and I sped quickly across Fountain, then over Fairfax to the Strip. The hotel was remarkably quiet, free from journalists and partiers and hangers-on. Nancy was in her bungalow, seated at Jock's desk correcting papers. I kissed her lightly and leaned over her shoulder. A freshman named Ed Shuttlesworth was getting a C-plus for his discussion of Kafka.

"I think I've figured it out."

She looked up at me and put down her pen.

"Frank Dichter murdered your husband."

"Frank Dichter? . . . Do you have any proof?"

"Nothing substantial. But I know why. Jock knew about Dichter's connection with a group of Cuban gangsters who run the Sexual Liberation League, an outfit that owns half the sex clubs in L.A., from the sleaziest massage parlor to the Liberation Institute. My guess is Dichter gave the Cubans the turf because they were old buddies from the Bay of Pigs invasion. That was probably all documented on a set of tapes Dichter stole from Jock after he murdered him. Dichter wanted them out of the way because Cubans are going out of style and he has his eye on higher office."

"How did Jock get these tapes?"

"I don't know."

"Are they still in existence?"

"Dichter destroyed them. He told me as much himself."

"I suppose he would . . . What about Deborah Frank?"

"I think he killed her too. They were both inside jobs, as

123

they say on TV."

Nancy smiled. "You mean they knew whoever killed them?"

"Either they knew him or he was famous enough to win their confidence."

"He or she."

"What?"

"He or she was famous enough. Women are famous too."

"Yeah . . . right." She was beginning to sound like Alora.

"But I don't understand. Why did he kill Deborah Frank?"

"She must have know something about the tapes. She was a media personality after all. She ran a talk show. She was dangerous."

"I thought she and Jock were feuding."

"Maybe they were. But that wouldn't prevent them using each other for publicity."

She looked at me skeptically. I didn't like the sound of it myself.

"So Dichter murdered her and then Jock and then Meiko as well, stuffing her in the air-conditioning duct of a sound stage at Twentieth Century Fox?"

"Yeah, well, I doubt that he did that part of it himself." The story was getting a little convoluted.

"Then who did?"

"That man we were chasing out in Topanga, maybe. They just dredged him out of the canyon. I heard it on the radio driving over here. He was working for the police."

"A plainclothesman?"

"Or a noclothesman . . . take your choice." I grinned at my own cheap joke, but she didn't think it was very funny.

"What does that prove? That the police were investigating the Liberation Institute?"

"Or trying to cover something up."

"Do you have any evidence of that?"

"Not yet."

"Then you don't have any hard evidence at all . . . implicating Dichter."

I shook my head.

"He's too important to make a blind accusation."

"Yeah, I know. I already tried that."

She turned away and resumed writing her comments on Ed Shuttlesworth's paper. I sat down on the sofa and looked at her. Her fingers were squeezed tight around the stub of a red pencil and her forehead was crinkled up as if she were concentrating harder than she needed.

"Of course there are always his alibis . . ."

"What about them?"

"They're pretty thin . . . When Jock was murdered he was allegedly sitting in his hotel room with his wife. When Deborah Frank was stabbed, he had some cockamamie excuse about having dinner with the Governor in Sacramento."

"Cockamamie?"

I reached for the phone. "Operator, in Sacramento, I'd like the telephone number of the *Bee*. That's the newspaper."

She gave me a number and I dialed direct. The switchboard operator connected me with the newsroom.

"Newsroom. Alberts speaking."

"Hello, Alberts. Is there anybody there who could tell me the whereabouts of Attorney General Frank Dichter on the night of Friday the 28th?"

"This is a newspaper. Not a research service."

"I know, but this is important. If you give me the right kind of information I can give you a scoop."

"What kind of scoop?"

"I can't say until you've given me the information, but I can promise it will be terriffic."

"Well, we don't —"

"If you don't tell me, I'll call the Los Angeles *Times*."

"All right . . . All right . . . Hold your noodle."

The mouthpiece of the phone clattered against a desk. In a few seconds, Alberts was back on the line.

"I don't know where he slept, but from about eight to eleven that night he was having dinner with the Governor at a place called the Yellow Fox on Jay Street."

"You sure about that?"

"Sure! There's a photo of the group right on the front page of the paper. The Governor and his wife, the Dichters and Art Linkletter with the champagne glasses on high. They're toasting a new campaign against teenage drug abuse."

I held up the phone and stared at it, counting the number of holes in the speaker. There were fifteen altogether, including a large one in the middle of the circle.

"You still there?"

"Yeah, I'm still here."

"What about the scoop?"

"There's no scoop. You gave me the wrong information."

I dropped the phone onto its cradle.

"It stuck, huh?" said Nancy.

I nodded and reached into my pocket for a joint. But I hadn't taken one with me. I stood and looked around the room. "Is there any more Wild Turkey? Or did Gunther drink it all?"

"There's another bottle over there." She pointed to the mantlepiece. I walked over and took a long swig. Then I sank down into the couch.

"Maybe he still did it," Nancy said. "Maybe he just had somebody kill Deborah and handled Jock himself."

"It's possible, I guess . . ."

"Or maybe it was somebody entirely different." She walked over and took the empty whiskey bottle out of my hand. "Somebody with a motive we haven't yet understood. She sat down on the couch next to me, our shoulders touching. Then she turned and kissed me. "I hope you get Dichter. He's a rat."

"I hope I do too." We stared at each other a few seconds. "You know I've been thinking about New York," I said.

"What about it?"

"Going there."

"Oh, come on."

"No, really. This detective business, it's lousy on the kids

126

I've got to get out of it before they get hurt."

"What's New York got to do with that?"

"I don't know. There are a lot of opportunities there for a guy with a B.A. in English and six months of law school."

"Like hot dog salesman in the 59th Street subway."

"That sounds good."

"You're crazy."

"Yeah, I guess I am . . . I guess it just bothers me."

"What?"

"Your going back to New York."

She didn't say anything.

"It makes me not want to get Dichter. It makes me want to stall as long as possible to keep you here."

"I'm leaving tomorrow."

I sat up and looked at her. "You're what?"

"Leaving tomorrow. In the afternoon. I have a class to teach."

"But . . ."

"But what?"

"Take a leave of absence. You're entitled to it under the circumstances."

"You *are* a romantic."

"Hey, now wait a minute! Not more than a day ago you told me I was the first guy except your husband you slept with in ten years."

"So?"

"Is that all it meant to you?"

"You're so old fashioned."

"Don't give me that horseshit. Is that all it meant to you?"

She didn't answer.

"What the hell is going on?"

"Nothing."

"Nothing?"

"Nothing . . . I'll try to stay."

"All right," I said.

I looked at her and frowned. She frowned back, but after a few seconds there was something about my grim expression she found very funny. She burst into laughter, wrapping her arms around me. I started to smile. We fell on the couch together and began to make terrific love. I didn't leave the bungalow until three in the morning.

18

I woke up to the sound of the Beach Boys singing "Surfin'
Safari." Jacob was playing it full volume on the stereo, dancing along in some seven-year-old's version of the boogaloo.
Ever since we saw *American Graffiti*, he had been getting
into fifties music with a vengeance. It was unnerving to
watch him thumb through my old albums, picking out the
Chuck Berry and Little Richard I had collected in junior high.

"Hey, Dad, where's your *Bo Diddley is a Gunslinger*? I
think it's lost."

"It's not lost . . . Now will you turn that thing off? I'm not
in the mood this morning."

"Okay, Pops." He shuffled over to the turntable and
pushed the reject button. "You sure are grouchy this
morning."

I pulled myself out of bed and walked into the bathroom,
gazing blearily into the mirror. I hadn't slept well, dreaming
and waking up. I had a mild headache and my eyes were
bloodshot. There were streaks of grey around my temples
and new creases were forming around my mouth. I was feeling old at thirty-one, a Now Generation has-been, as shopworn as any of the old soldiers in the coffee house in Topanga. If Gunther was going to put me on the cover of *Rolling
Stone*, he'd better do it soon, before I lost my appeal to the

129

youth market.

I turned on the shower and let the water warm up, watching Jacob on the floor of the living room studying the liner notes of a frayed Buddy Holly album, his lips sounding out the words.

"Do you want to go to New York?" I asked him, but he didn't hear me over the rushing water.

I tested it and stepped inside, standing there without soaping up, letting the drops wash over me. It was obvious what was bothering me. I didn't want Nancy to go yet. I hardly knew her but already I was feeling rejected. It was as if she didn't give a damn anymore. It didn't matter who killed her husband. It wasn't significant, not part of their marriage contract as published in the charter issue of *Ms.* magazine.

It made me angry. I'd show her, I thought, reaching for the soap and lathering up all over. Another inadvertent erection appeared, but I ignored it. I had overlooked a few things, that was clear. I hadn't thoroughly examined the interplay between the two murders. In fact, I didn't have the faintest idea why Deborah Frank was stabbed to death.

I rinsed off the cold water and thought about going over to the Beverly Wilshire to have a look at the scene of the crime. But what would that prove? I had read the newspaper reports. And besides, the police had already combed every inch of the room, and what they might have left was certainly cleaned out by now, the room taken over by its new occupant, some visiting dignitary from the Italian film industry, probably — Dino de something or other — or some free-spending Texas businessman.

No. There had to be some other approach. What had Jock said in his suicide note? What motivation had been imputed to him by his murderer. He had been "unable to achieve my goal." The gap between his principles and actions had widened "beyond any possible rectification." And what were his principles? Sexual freedom. And what was his goal? Liberation. But what did that have to do with the murder of Deborah Frank?

I shut off the shower and stepped out onto the mat, drying myself with a beach towel and staring at the poster of the Marx Brothers taped to the bathroom door. Then I walked into the living room, picked up the phone and dialed the Marmont.

"Chateau Marmont . . . Good morning, dearie."

"No joking around this morning, Grace. Just get me bungalow five."

"All right . . . All right . . . Just a minute."

The phone rang six times. I was already beginning to sweat when Nancy picked up on the seventh.

"Hello."

"How are you?" I said.

"How am I! Moses, do you know what time it is?"

"Seven fifteen."

"Jesus! What do you want?"

"I just wanted to be sure you were . . . still here."

"I'm here."

"I'm glad. Don't leave . . . okay?"

She didn't answer.

"Nancy?"

"Yeah."

"I'll call you later."

I hung up and went and made the kids breakfast — whole wheat pancakes with yeast and non-fat milk. It was my contribution to good health. Then I went and made another phone call. This time the recipient was an early-riser like me.

"Good morning . . . and may this be the first day of the rest of your life!"

"Good morning, Cindy. This is Moses Wine."

"Oh, Moses, how good to hear from you. I hope this is to say you're coming back to visit us at the Institute. It's unfair you had your first look under such inconvenient circumstances."

"Yeah, well, I was actually calling for a little help."

"Moses, you know I'm always ready to help people live up to their human potential."

"Not that kind of help, Cindy. It's about Jock. I'm still trying to piece things together."

"About what?"

"About Jock. The murders. Remember? Jock Hecht and Deborah Frank."

There was a silence.

"You still there?"

"Yes, of course. I'm always here."

"Then tell me what you know."

"Oh, my God. That was terrible, wasn't it?"

"What?"

"The cop nosing around here the other day."

"Yeah."

"He got what he deserved."

"Yeah, uh, Cindy —"

"Always the forces of reaction are against us, Moses, trying to bring down the truly liberated."

"I know what you mean. Look, Cindy . . ."

"I don't know anything about Jock, Moses. I don't ever want to know!"

"Was Deborah Frank ever up there with him?"

"She might have been. We don't say who visits the Institute. That would be unprofessional."

"Who would say? The League?"

"Now don't get nasty."

"All right, Cindy." I was beginning to get fed up. "I don't think you know who your friends really are. Suppose I were to tell you that the real owner of your sainted Institute was the Attorney General of this state and that in all probability he would like nothing better than to shut it down in short order. What would you think of that?"

"It . . . um . . . sounds a little wild, but, um —"

"But, um, try it on the gang in the sauna and see how it washes."

Again she was silent.

"All I'm asking is a small hint, a clue. A woman in your position hears many things. A stiff cock has no conscience, as my grandfather used to say."

"How quaint. But in truth, I don't know anything. Though I can tell you this, Moses. If there's one person who knows all there is to know about Jock Hecht, more even than his . . . beloved Nancy, it's Marcia Lynn . . ."

"Who's that?"

"His agent . . . at World Management Associates."

"Thanks, Cindy. You're a pal. If I know anybody with primary or secondary dysfunction, I'll send him to you straight away."

I hung up and got the kids ready to go, fixing Jacob's lunch and collecting some extra diapers for Simon. Then I gathered them together and headed for the door.

We were halfway out when a letter fell through the slot. It looked like junk mail and there was no telling how long it had been sitting there, but I reached down for it and opened it anyway. I was sorry I did.

A Unique Experience Awaits You At
Los Angeles' Only

HOUSE OF DOMINANCE

3218 Vista del Mar, Redondo Beach
Discreet appointments advised — 463-3848

"At the sign of the claw!"

A pair of whips was crossed beneath a cat's claw at the bottom. Someone had scrawled "See Dolores — she delivers!" over the top in magenta lipstick.

I groaned and shoved the letter in my hip pocket.

19

"Ms. Lynn is in a meeting."

"When will this meeting be over?"

"At eleven. When she begins her second meeting with Gore Vidal and Sam Peckinpah."

"And after that?"

"She has her conference with David Lean, Warren Beatty and Lawrence Durrell."

"And then?"

"She goes to lunch with the vice-president of Paramount Pictures and the editor-in-chief of Simon & Schuster."

"What's she doing after lunch?"

"After lunch she is flying to London for a week."

The receptionist at World Management Associates gazed across her Selectric with a smile of utmost condescension.

"Does Ms. Lynn take time out to shit?"

"Ms. Lynn is totally unavailable."

I backed up and paced around the waiting room. A nervous young actress was seated on a gold velour sofa, waiting to be called in by one of the agents. She glanced up at me, trying to decide if I was important enough to smile at, then turned away. I stared past her at a bust of Conrad Epstein, the mustachioed gentleman who founded the agency in 1898. Even in bronze, he had the bland, seemingly disinterested expression of a vicious poker player.

"May I use your phone?" I asked the receptionist.

"Is it long distance?"

"Just as far as the Fox lot."

"Use eight," she said, pushing it in my direction.

She looked annoyed as I pulled the phone around into a corridor and dialed the studio number, asking for extension 312.

"Hello, Gruskow. This is Moses Wine."

"Oh, hello, Moses. Jeez, we're still stuck on that gangster film. Lars is threatening to go back to Malmö."

"I know how it is . . . Listen, how much clout do you have in the motion picture business?"

"Well, some people say —"

"I mean real clout. Muscle."

"I'm all right."

"Can you get me in to see Marcia Lynn?"

"Sure."

"I mean right now. In the next five minutes."

"Well . . ."

"No fucking around, Gruskow. This is the real thing. If you can do it, you have me as an unpaid consultant for life. Anything you want to know. Detectives, gangsters, police, the works. I'll even introduce you to a gay bookie who claims to have shot the ex-president of Argentina."

"But —"

"Five minutes, Gruskow."

I hung up the phone and put the receiver back on the desk. Then I stood at the end of the corridor watching the trainees rush back and forth to the mail room, manila envelopes clutched to their chests in grim self-importance.

Three minutes later, the receptionist tapped me on the shoulder. "Ms. Lynn will see you now."

"It's about time."

I followed her down the corridor, the young actress looking up surprisedly as we passed.

Ms. Lynn was not in her office when the receptionist opened the door. I took a seat in a black leather Eames chair and looked around. It was a large, homey room filled with potted plants. Ferns and *Ficus benjamina.* The walls were covered with photographs of famous clients. I recognized one of Hecht at the National Book Award ceremony and another of him at an International PEN Conference in Vienna, standing with a tennis racket next to Heinrich Böll. Before I had finished looking them all over, Marcia Lynn entered and sat down opposite me without saying a word. She was an imposing woman in her forties with long, burnt sienna hair and an orange scarf around her neck. In her hand she held a box of Balkan Sobranies.

"You're working for Nancy Hecht," she said. "You have my sympathies. Such a difficult woman."

"Difficult?"

"Married to a man of genius. It always creates problems. I've seen it time and again."

"What have you seen?"

"Misunderstandings."

I gave her a questioning look.

"Don't be so puzzled, Mr. Wine. It's quite obvious. I warned her. You don't marry a man like that without knowing what you're getting into. Geniuses have their own imperatives. They're not bound by conventional morality. We've known that for generations. Marlowe and Kyd in that tavern brawl. Rimbaud and Verlaine. Baudelaire. Genet. If we applied our standards to those people, our literature would be reduced to trivia — not to mention our art, music and even science."

"You have a high opinion of Jock Hecht, Ms. Lynn."

"High? I wouldn't say that. Jock never had a chance to realize his potential. I feel certain that the new book would have been his best book. A masterpiece. He was risking personal exposure akin to . . . Boswell in *The London Journal.*"

"What kind of exposure?"

"Humiliation. Ridicule by Philistines . . . He was investigating the very nature of our sexuality, the very . . ." She stopped herself and gazed up maternally at the National Book Award photo. "The very essence of human need." She lit her cigarette and blew out, as if to emphasize the statement. Jock Hecht might have been dead, but Marcia Lynn had not stopped being his agent.

"About Nancy Hecht," I asked. "Why do you think she was so difficult?"

"Naiveté, my dear. She thought she'd married a soulmate, someone who'd sit up with her all night analyzing Proust and accompany her to chamber music concerts. She should have married another professor for that, not an artist."

"I thought they had good communication in their marriage."

"Naturally."

"With permission to sleep with others."

"And how!"

"And a marriage contract."

"Well, of course," she laughed again. "I know all about that. I wrote it!"

"You wrote it?"

"Well, practically. Not the words of course. She wrote them. But it was my suggestion. Jock had an anthology of his early fiction coming out then. The first issue of *Ms.* wanted something sensational; but she took it so seriously, poor thing."

"So would I," I said. She gave me a sharp look but I jumped quickly into the breach before she decided to terminate our interview.

"Was Jock working on something, some bit of muckraking to go along with the personal experience?"

"What do you mean?"

"An exposé, perhaps."

"What kind?"

"I don't know. Some research into the porno business."

"I tend to doubt it. But he stumbled onto things all the time."

"What about Deborah Frank? Did you know her?"

"Certainly."

137

"Well?"

"Quite well."

She had a wry smile on her face and was staring at the wall behind my head. I turned and followed her gaze to a large, color photograph of the late Deborah Frank. She was standing in front of a television camera holding a clipboard. Her hair and eyes were dark and she had dark skin; she looked like a perfect Jewish princess, the way I imagined Queen Esther when I was a little boy in Sunday school. On the bottom she had written: "To my Marcia — Where would I be without you?"

"So you were her agent."

"Indeed I am."

"Hers and Jock's?"

"That's correct."

"Didn't that create difficulties?"

"Of course not. Jock recommended me to her."

"Jock recommended you?"

"Writers do that all the time. I don't normally have television personalities for clients. I'm a literary agent. But we got along splendidly."

"You got along splendidly! But Jock —"

There was a buzz from her secretary. Mr. Vidal and Mr. Peckinpah were waiting outside.

"I'm sorry, Mr. Wine. But I must ask you to leave. I hope I've been helpful."

"Wait a minute. A couple of more questions. I don't understand this . . . I thought Jock and Deborah Frank were feuding."

"I don't want to talk about it."

"Why not?"

"That doesn't matter, Mr. Wine. I said I didn't want to talk about it."

"Then they weren't feuding."

"Well . . ."

"There are only two alternatives, Ms. Lynn. Either they were feuding or they weren't."

"Is that so?"

"And I say they weren't. I say it was a hoax."

"What on earth for?"

"Publicity, of course."

"And who would have dreamed up something like that?"

"The only person with something to gain from both ends. Their agent."

She walked around the desk and held the door open for me. I could see the celebrities outside waiting for her. She flashed a charming smile.

"One more thing. How long had Deborah Frank been your client?"

"We met two years ago."

"When Jock was working on the Jewish mafia book?"

"That's right."

"Then they met through Meyer Greenglass . . ."

"I don't know, Mr. Wine."

"She's his niece."

"So I've been told . . ."

"It would make sense."

"Perhaps . . . Good day, Mr. Wine." She walked past me into the outstretched arms of Sam Peckinpah.

20

"Where's the tapes?"

Instant replay! I had just sat down at the wheel of the rented Vega when I felt an arm about as thick as a sewer pipe wrapping around my neck and yanking upwards. I wasn't able to get out an answer until he had repeated the question.

"Where're the tapes?"

"The tapes don't exist!"

"Bullshit!"

I was pulled up, back over the seat and thrown face down on the floor of the car. A fist like a lead ingot slammed into my back inches above the kidneys.

"Where's the tapes?"

"You're getting a little monotonous, pal."

"Where are they?" He let me have it again with his lead fist.

"They're destroyed. Everybody knows that!"

"Likely story."

"Hey, c'mon, don't you Cubans know when to lay off?"

"I'm no fuckin' Cuban!" And gave it to me again.

I turned my head and looked just to verify that it was true. He was no fucking Cuban. He was a blond Anglo about the size of Godzilla.

He raised his fist again and I threw up my hands in self-defense. "Hey, if you lay off, I'll tell you what I told the Cubans!"

He stopped and I had about six seconds to explain myself. The truth was as good as anything.

"Those tapes were stolen by Attorney General Frank Dichter and destroyed as soon as he got ahold of them."

That stopped him.

"Get up!" said the man.

I struggled to my knees and pulled myself up the back of the seat. When I reached the top, he bashed me on the chin and sent me sprawling to the floor again, my feet dangling over the hatchback. Then he picked me up and started to do it once more when I slammed him a quick one in the ribs. I followed up with a chop to the neck and a hard kick in the right side of his groin. He doubled over and I was about to finish him, when he pulled a .38 from under his jacket and pushed it against my forehead, jabbing me in the solar plexus with his other hand.

"All right," I said. "I get the picture. But you can slice out my left eye and run over my balls with a power mower and I still won't tell you where the tapes are because I don't know. And if I'm dead, I'm sure as hell not going to tell you."

"My instructions are to get those tapes from you!"

"Who gave you those instructions?"

"None of your fucking business!" He picked me up by the collar again, twisting my neck against the steering wheel.

"Hey, man, how about a compromise? I'm looking for the tapes. You're looking for the tapes. We have a lot in common. Why don't you just follow me around and when I find them they're yours!"

Godzilla looked at me, considering. He had a scar across the bridge of his nose, which had been twisted sideways as if he had a deviated septum. Once he must have run into somebody bigger than he was. Maybe Wilt Chamberlain.

We stared at each other for a while longer. He was debating with himself about what to do, but was having some trouble with it. It was like watching a dinosaur, an outsized

141

body with a peanut-sized brain. I had about given up that he would ever come to a decision when he put his gun away and got out of the car.

I sat down behind the wheel and touched my face. Blood was trickling out of my nose and my jaw felt tender. In the rear-view mirror, I could see my blond friend settling down at the driver's seat of a black Buick. I backed up and drove out of the lot with him right behind me. Apparently I was going to have company. I had to smile. Where I was going next was sure to make him nervous.

It was already afternoon as I hurtled down the Harbor Freeway toward the prison. This time Greenglass would have to see me. This time the cat and mouse game was over. He'd been sitting behind bars for too long, silent as a Second Avenue Buddha, when I was certain he knew the answers that could tie this thing together.

The Buick stayed right behind me, two lengths back, as I sped past the Cal State campus at Dominguez Hills. Deborah Frank, Greenglass, Jock Hecht, Dichter. Nancy, Cynthia Hardwick, Marcia Lynn, Santiago Martin. Their names and faces whirled in front of my eyes. Gruskow's and Gunther's too, I couldn't forget them. Or Meiko either. Was she greedy, like Santiago had said, or just an unlucky masseuse? And what about Deborah Frank and Jock? Were they really pals . . . lovers ever? They got together through Greenglass and then with Marcia Lynn. But why pretend they were fighting? Why make such a public display? For a book? To expose the tapes together? And how did Hecht get the tapes in the first place?

And who was this reject from the guard tower at Auschwitz who was pinned to my tail? Didn't anybody tell him the tapes were erased? It was a shame to be so out of touch, such a social reject, the only one at a cocktail party who hadn't seen *The Exorcist*.

I turned off the freeway at San Pedro, sinking deeper into the seat and feeling the card from the House of Dominance in my hip pocket. That, too, was peculiar. I couldn't figure out how, all of a sudden, I had gotten on the dirty-old-man list for that kind of thing. Jesus, do they get your name automatically when you turn thirty-one? And who would have the weird sense of humor to scribble "See Dolores — she delivers" over the top in real lipstick? Some cheap whore in Redondo Beach? It didn't make sense.

I turned again, the sky remaining clear as I crossed the bridge spanning the harbor to Terminal Island. The rain had swept the sky clean and it had stayed that way, the coast of Catalina still visible to the right with the skyline of Long Beach up ahead, each building etched against the blue. I could even make out the larger yachts moored along the Gold Coast of Orange County, their multicolored banners waving proudly above the marinas. It was as if the gods had given the city a second chance, had erased the last forty years and told us we could try again. But we'd better not muck it up this time.

I continued along the rim of Terminal Island, past the tuna cannery, the Coast Guard station, the Portuguese sailor bars, to the gate of the federal prison. The inmates were out in force, mowing the lawns and trimming the hedges. Godzilla pulled over to the side and parked as the guard signaled me through to the administration offices.

The associate warden didn't look overjoyed to see me. It was a busy day, he said, government inspectors were coming through. A congressman from the 12th District and someone from HEW. Besides, Greenglass hadn't been feeling well lately. He had been sick.

"Sick?" I asked. "He looked okay to me."

"He's been ailing, off and on."

"What's wrong?"

"That's his business."

But Greenglass wasn't willing to talk about it. In fact, he wasn't willing to talk with me about anything at all.

"There's no way you can prevail upon him . . . just for a minute?"

The warden had started to usher me out.

143

"No way at all."

"But this is crucial. He has information that could lead to the solution of a crime."

"Doubtless he has information that could lead to the solution of many crimes."

"Multiple murder," I said.

"Good-bye, Mr. Wine."

A guard stood at the door waiting for me to leave.

Feeling frustrated and depressed, I walked down the ramp to the prison grounds. A group of black inmates was playing baseball in the yard. A guy with hair like Sly Stone was at the plate. He missed the first pitch but lined the second one cleanly between the shortstop and the third-baseman. It bounced on the cement past the left-fielder, over a small guard rail and across the lawn where some other prisoners were playing chess, then rolled toward a grove of Washington palms. In front of the grove, on a wooden bench, an old man huddled in a grey blanket, though the temperature was climbing into the middle seventies. It was Greenglass.

Under the eyes of a guard, I headed in his direction. When I reached the rail I was stopped by another guard. I stood there staring at the old Jew from a hundred feet off. His complexion had turned an institutional green. His skin was layered with wrinkles like drippings down a candle.

"Mr. Greenglass! Mr. Greenglass! I have to talk with you!"

He didn't say anything.

"Mr. Greenglass, it's about Jock Hecht and your niece Debbie. You must talk to me."

He still did not respond.

"Mr. Greenglass!"

He did not move or turn in any way. I wondered if he could hear me. I tried a last time.

"Greenglass, you *momzer*, come clean. What went on between Hecht and Debbie Frank?"

Still nothing. A wind came up, riffling the palm trees. The beginnings of a Santa Ana. The left-fielder ran past Greenglass, retrieving a baseball. From behind, I could hear another

144

guard coming up to throttle me. I knew this was it, but I didn't want to leave.

Then Greenglass raised his hand and beckoned to the baseball player. The black youth stopped — he couldn't have been more than twenty-two — and walked over to the old man. They stood there together for a moment, a frozen cameo of American life. Greenglass said a few words. The left-fielder nodded. Greenglass took out a piece of paper and wrote something on it. He handed it to the youth and pointed in my direction.

The left-fielder took it and headed toward me. "From the Zionist pig," he said, slapping the paper in my hand. I opened it and read: "(212) 948-3652. Ask for Bathsheba." I tried to memorize the number before the guard could take it away.

Godzilla was waiting for me.

We drove off the island belly-to-belly, as if we were locked in a Labor Day traffic jam. In my rear-view mirror, I could see the goon hunched over his steering wheel, his bashed-in nose protruding toward the windshield. I had to decide whether I should shake him before I slipped into a booth to phone New York.

I studied his cold, grey eyes. They were empty pools, the valueless orbs of the good soldier in the cause of murder, the kind that always carried out orders from the top, never flinched even if it came to strangling babies or dropping bombs on peasant villages. William Calley eyes. Twentieth-century eyes. They chilled me, but they were beneath contempt.

I continued over the bridge, paying the toll on the San Pedro side and driving into the shopping area. Godzilla stayed right behind me, not shirking his duty for a moment, never dreaming his orders had implications.

Implications. As I pulled into a Standard station, I suddenly had the feeling I hadn't studied the implications of the case myself. There were other permutations, combinations. Suppose I had misread Greenglass and he was leading me down a primrose path of some sort — not really as inno-

145

cent as he appeared to be "proving." Suppose, indeed, Dichter hadn't murdered Jock at all. Or Debbie. Or Meiko. Then what?

I got out of the car and crossed in front of Godzilla's Buick, tapping it on the hood. He reached for the door handle.

"Don't get excited," I said. "I just had a hunch about the fourth at Hollywood Park and I've got to check with my bookie."

He sat back uneasily and watched. I entered the booth and dropped a dime in the slot, billing the long distance to my home phone when I contacted the operator.

"948-3652." A woman with an English accent answered in a tone that was pompous and efficient.

"I'd like to speak with Bathsheba."

"Who is calling?"

"My name is Moses Wine."

"Does Bathsheba know you?"

"No, she doesn't. I'm a friend of Meyer Greenglass."

"I don't believe I'm acquainted with a Mr. Greenglass."

"Well, she is . . . Ask her."

"One moment."

I heard a little argument in the background before the English woman returned to the phone. I was beginning to suspect she was a housekeeper or governess of some sort.

"Bathsheba does not know this Mr. Greenglass."

"But I'm sure —"

"She's never heard of him."

"Listen, this is important. I really must speak with her. Just for a minute."

"I have no way of knowing who you are, sir."

"Listen, to whom am I speaking?"

There was a click at the other end.

I stared down Godzilla and tried again, this time placing the call person-to-person to Bathsheba. It wasn't accepted.

I walked out into the Standard station, getting dizzy from the gas fumes and afternoon sun. There had to be some better way to get through to this woman; but even if I could, I

146

had no sense of what to ask her or what she would tell me.

It was three o'clock and I drove back into the city again, veering from the Harbor Freeway onto the Hollywood and then off at Echo Park Avenue. I headed straight for my house and parked in front, Godzilla behind me. I went directly inside, shut the door for a second and then stuck my head out again.

"I've got the tapes," I said, watching him jump eagerly out of the driver's side of his car. I tossed a spool of cellophane at his feet. "April fool," I said and slammed the door in his face.

Then I sat down in front of the telephone and dialed the New York number directly. Lo and behold, it was Bathsheba who answered. She had a sweet, high-pitched voice and I guessed she was about nine.

"Hello, Bathsheba, my name is Moses Wine."

"I know who you are. You're a detective. You're working for my mom. She told me about you on the phone."

"Did she?"

"Yesterday . . . I'm sorry I didn't talk with you, but old Spreckles is so stuffy. She wouldn't tell me who you were until after you'd hung up. She thought you were one of those, you know, nasty callers."

"I'm not nasty. At least I don't think I am."

"You sound okay to me."

I may have sounded okay, but I wasn't feeling that way. I slumped deeper into the couch, feeling distinctly unnerved, as if I were Alice plunging unwittingly through the looking glass.

"What did your mom say I was doing?" I asked.

"Helping her."

"Helping her what?"

"Helping her find out about my dad."

"Find out what?"

"If he was murdered or if he committed suicide."

Her voice hardly quavered. She had been well-trained by Miss Spreckles.

147

"What do you think happened?"

"I don't know . . . How should I know?"

"What does your mom think?"

"She doesn't know either."

"Do you know a man named Meyer Greenglass?"

"No."

"Or Frank Dichter?"

"No."

"Or Santiago Martin?"

"No."

"Or a woman named Deborah Frank?"

"No."

"Have you ever heard of any of these people?"

"No."

"What about Sal Gruskow, Cynthia Hardwick or Gunther Thomas?"

"No, no and no . . . Why are you asking me all of these questions?"

"I don't know."

"That's not a very good reason."

"It surely isn't . . . because somebody told me to."

"Who?"

"Meyer Greenglass."

"But I don't know him."

"He was a friend of your dad's."

"Did you know my father?" she asked.

"I met him."

"Did you think he was a great man?"

I didn't know how to answer that. I sat there silently for a while, holding the phone and feeling myself plunge deeper and deeper through the looking glass. My eyes shut and I watched myself spin hand over foot through a dark void. Bathsheba's voice interrupted my daydream.

"Are you still there, Mr. Wine?"

"Yes, I'm here."

"I miss my mom."

"I bet you do. She's a fine woman."

"We couldn't go to the children's concert today."

"She'll be back soon."

"I know. She's coming back tonight after I'm asleep."

"She is?"

"Spreckles told me."

"Then I guess she is."

"She's been away since last Friday."

"You mean since Saturday. She's been gone since Saturday."

"No, no. Since Friday. I didn't go to school that afternoon when we dropped her off at the airport."

"To go where? San Francisco?"

"No. Los Angeles. To be with my dad."

"But . . ." I searched for something to say, but I couldn't complete the sentence. My heart was palpitating and my hands were getting clammy. I stared at the phone. It was melting like a Dali before my eyes.

"Mr. Wine?"

"Yes, Bathsheba."

"Do you have any more questions you want to ask me?"

"No, Bathsheba. No, I don't."

"I hope I'll meet you sometime." She was really charming. The way things were going, Jacob could call her in ten years . . .

"Maybe you will." I could barely get the words out. "Tell Spreckles to take good care of you, Bathsheba. Good night."

I hung up the phone, then took out some papers and started to roll a joint. But I put the pack back in my vest pocket and walked back slowly to the car feeling depressed.

21

"We don't give out that information, sir, unless authorized."

"I'm not horsing around, shmuck!" I grabbed the desk clerk at the Marmont by his narrow, black tie and twisted hard.

"Whaa?"

"You heard me! Now where is she?"

"She left for the airport."

"How long ago?"

"Twenty minutes."

"How did she go? Did she take the limousine?"

"I don't know, sir."

"Well, think, you asshole. Think"

"I think she took it, sir. Yes."

"What line did she take?"

"I wouldn't know, sir."

"You wouldn't know?"

The desk clerk nodded nervously.

"You sure?"

"I swear."

I released my grip and he fell over backward onto the counter, rubbing his neck. I stormed out of the lobby and jumped into my car, speeding out to the airport.

150

It was rush hour and the traffic was stacked all up and down Century Boulevard. I crawled along looking for Nancy, running through in my head all the airlines that flew to New York — American, United, TWA. The first one I came to was United. I pulled over into the passenger loading zone and ran inside. Nancy wasn't in the waiting room and they didn't have a plane going to New York for another two hours.

I tried TWA. The passengers were already boarding on their five o'clock flight. I glanced at the list for Nancy's name. She wasn't among them. I ran out of the building down the block to American Airlines. The waiting room was jampacked with people. Chicago, New York, Boston — there was a long list of flights flashing across the closed circuit television. Several limousines were parked by the curb. I pushed through the crowd, trying to find her, making a circle between the lobby and the baggage claim area and back again. The loudspeaker announced a flight for Atlanta and another bound for Houston. A group of backpackers pushed past me, carrying their gear over to the check-in counter.

I stopped and took a breath. I thought of trying United again when I saw her, fifty yards off, riding along the moving sidewalk toward the embarkation gates, an overnight bag under her arm.

I stepped onto the sidewalk and walked swiftly up behind her. When I was ten feet away, she sensed my presence and turned around.

"Oh, hello," she said.

"Hello."

"You didn't have to come to the airport. I mean, it really wasn't necessary."

"It wasn't?"

"I told you I was going back to New York. I have to. I've missed two classes already."

She waited for me to react, but I just stood there, a couple of steps away from her on the moving belt.

"Good-bye," she said and kissed me on the cheek.

We came to the end of the belt. She gave me an apprehensive look and headed for the escalator at the gates, but I grabbed hold of her wrist before she could start up.

"Hey, what's going on?" She forced a smile. "A brute display of male strength? Marriage by capture? I didn't think you were so old fashioned."

"Where were you on Friday night?"

"What are you talking about?"

"Just what I said. Where were you on Friday night?"

"I don't understand."

"Can't you answer a simple question?"

"I have to make a plane." She tried to wrench herself free, but I held fast.

"Where were you?" I repeated.

She hesitated. "In New York, I guess . . . I don't know."

"You guess? That was four days ago."

"So much has happened. I can't keep it straight."

"Let me refresh your memory. Your daughter Bathsheba says she dropped you at the airport on Friday afternoon."

"Bathsheba?"

"You were on your way here. With the three-hour time difference, you were in Los Angeles by six o'clock, give or take an hour."

"What's that supposed to mean?"

"You didn't meet me until twenty-four hours later, only minutes after I discovered Jock's body. And I thought you had just stepped off a plane."

The loudspeaker announced the last call for the flight to New York. Nancy turned away, facing the escalator.

"Where were you, Nancy?"

"I've really got to go, Moses."

"Tell me, Nancy. You have to tell me."

"I'll call you from New York. We can straighten it out."

"How do I know you'll call?"

"What?"

"How do I know you'll even stay in New York?"

"What is this? An interrogation? I thought you were working for me."

"Nancy, just explain it to me. Then it'll all be over and you can go on your merry way."

I turned around, forcing her to look at me again. She averted her eyes.

"Nancy, come on."

"Come on what?"

"Help us both out of this thing!"

"What if I can't?"

I released her and took a step away. A pair of nuns carrying briefcases walked past us and headed onto the escalator.

"I think we'd better go," I said.

"All right."

I took her arm and without speaking we walked together down the corridor to the passenger loading zone. Another limousine was moving out as we got into the car. I shut the doors and we drove off, out of the airport and up along Century Boulevard.

"Where're we going?" she asked.

"What does it matter?"

The sun was setting behind us; a grey, cold fog knifing in from the ocean. I stopped at a light and looked at her.

"Where'd you go on Friday, Nancy, when you arrived in Los Angeles?"

She didn't say anything.

"To the Beverly Wilshire Hotel?"

She nodded.

"Debbie Frank's room?"

She nodded again.

The light turned green, but there was no point in driving on. I pulled over to the curb and parked. In the reflection of a street lamp, I could see her profile. She was biting her lip, restraining tears.

"Why'd you do it, Nancy?"

"I didn't mean to. It all came out. I only wanted to trap them together."

"And he wasn't there; he was with Meiko."

"I didn't expect that. When I found Deborah alone, she said it was all over between Jock and me. That she was going to marry him. That he never loved me. That was why he wanted the open marriage in the first place, she said, because he was bored with me."

"And you believed that?"

"No. But I did know there was something special between them. He had always told me everything, every little minute detail of his affairs. That was the way it was supposed to be. It was written in our contract. You could do anything you wanted as long as you told the other person. But he never told me about Deborah. He went to incredible lengths to keep it a secret, manufacturing that phony competition and lying about her all the time."

"What'd she say?"

"She said I was naive, that he had many affairs he never told me about, that the contract was just so much paper and that I was a fool."

"What'd you do?"

"I didn't do anything . . . The table in her hotel room was set for two, with a bottle of French champagne. She said Jock was coming when he finished his research with Meiko, that they would eat and then they would run away together."

"Was she telling the truth?"

"I don't know. There were bags on the bed . . . She just sat there, grinning at me. I wanted to leave, but I was transfixed. Then Jock came."

"What's he say?"

"Nothing."

"Nothing?"

A bus roared by, rattling the car windows. Nancy hesitated, fighting to hold herself together. "He . . . he just came in and kissed me hello as if it were the most normal thing in the world. Then he hugged and kissed Deborah in front of me, sticking his hand in the back of her skirt and clutching her to him. I didn't know how to react. I pulled him away, demanding an explanation, but he wouldn't give me any. He took us both by the hand instead and led us over to the bed. I didn't want to go, but he kept tugging at me till I broke free. I backed across the room, upset, shouting at him that he had broken the contract. But he and Deborah just smiled. They told me to stop being so hung-up, so possessive, to relax and liberate my body. Then they stood and came toward me again, smiling, hugging and caressing me, trying to take my clothes off. They started to undress, fondling each other in front of the mirror. Licking each other's lips. Touching each other's genitals. Jock reached for me, but I wouldn't go . . . I couldn't stand it . . . I . . . I started throwing things, picking up silverware and glasses, yelling and screaming. But they weren't listening to me anymore . . . lost in each other's excitement . . . lost . . . touching . . . holding . . . Then Deborah fell to her knees, taking Jock's penis in her hand, opening her mouth. He went inside. Thrusting. It was horrible. 'No!' I shouted. But they couldn't hear me. They . . . they . . . I didn't . . . I screamed and ran to the table, picked up the knife . . . I didn't know what I was doing . . . didn't know . . . I . . . I . . ."

I put my arm around her and pulled her to me, holding her to my chest while she sobbed. The sun had all but disappeared and the ocean fog was enshrouding us, the green neon of a liquor store blinking in the distance. A wino stumbled out of the door with a bottle of Muscatel and hobbled off into the night. I closed my eyes and tried not to think of what had happened, tried just to think of Nancy's body next to mine. I squeezed my lids even tighter, hoping to erase everything, hoping it would all be gone when I opened them again.

It didn't work. But when I did open them, I almost laughed, I saw something so comically sordid in my rear-view mirror. It was Godzilla parked not more than ten feet behind us, hunched like some monstrous dark angel at his steering wheel.

I started the motor and drove off. Nancy didn't move, leaving her head against my chest. In a while, I could feel the water of her tears soaking through my shirt.

"Are you going to take me in?" she asked.

"Not now."

I turned left and wound my way up La Cienega.

"Where're we going then?"

"Back to the Marmont. I want you to take back your old bungalow, lock the door and stay there until you hear from me."

She nodded. I ran my hand through her hair.

"Why did you want me to take this case?"

"After it happened . . . I was feeling so guilty. I wanted to know whether Jock committed suicide or not. Then when you found out Dichter killed him, I wanted to go back to New York before you —"

"Dichter didn't do it." She looked up at me, puzzled. "Jock killed himself . . . He sent me a message from the dead."

I took the envelope from my hip pocket and showed it to her. She didn't know what to make of it.

Then I let her off and sped away. I had to move fast. There wasn't enough time to cry.

22

Every time I go to Redondo Beach I think of the Beach Boys. In my mind, they are as closely associated with that town as Mozart with Salzburg or Wagner with Bayreuth. So I hummed "Help Me, Rhonda" to myself to keep my equilibrium as I drove south along the Coast Highway past Playa del Rey.

Behind me, Godzilla was perplexed, wondering what I was doing out here in the middle of the night cruising along in a deserted beach city. *Help me, Rhonda. Help, help me, Rhonda. Help me, Rhonda. Help, help me, Rhonda. Help me, Rhonda, yeah, get her out of my heart!*

I stopped at a Denny's by the waterfront and stepped into the phone booth. The image of the cigarette burns on Meiko's back kept popping into my head as I made first one phone call and then another, arranging a showdown. Godzilla watched suspiciously from the counter. Outside I could hear the mournful beep of the foghorn and the waves crashing against the pier.

My shadow walked over to the booth and pulled the door open.

"Who're you talking to?" he queried.

"It's on for tonight."

"What?"

"Ever get beaten by a leather strap while you ejaculated?"

"Huh?"

"Or burned with a cigarette while you were frenching a woman?"

"I don't get it."

"You don't get it?"

"Nah."

"You should try everything once. That's what Jock Hecht told me . . . Come on!"

We headed out of the coffee shop and onto the street by the pier, continuing down the cement boardwalk like the Monster and Dr. Frankenstein. We were alone on the ocean front. The fog had enveloped everything, leaving only the halos around the street lamps and a few dimly lit windows in the beach houses. We passed several narrow streets debouching onto the sand and then turned right on Vista del Mar, a dilapidated street lined with clapboard houses that looked scheduled for demolition. The House of Dominance was at the end, the last outpost of sexual flim-flam.

We walked up and knocked on the door.

"This a whorehouse?" asked Godzilla.

"Not exactly."

"What do you mean 'not exactly'?"

"Chances are they don't do anything, really, but put up a show and take your money."

"Then I ain't goin' in."

"Suit yourself," I said. "But you may be missing more than you think."

Godzilla shot me another suspicious look. I knocked on the door again. No one answered.

Godzilla grabbed me by the shirt. "Hey, you tryin' to pull somethin'?"

"What do you mean?"

"This place ain't even open!" He pointed at a "For Sale" sign in front of the building. In the fog, I hadn't even seen it

"I see what you mean," I said.

"Now what's going on here, you little Jewish cocksucker!"

"Nothing special."

"What the fuck are you talkin' about? You lead me all the way out here to the middle of nowhere and you say there's nothin' goin' on?"

"They're paying you to follow me, aren't they?"

"They're payin' me to bring back the tapes!"

He picked me up and tried to throw me against the wall of the building. I slumped to the ground, hearing a loud, cracking noise that was either my ribs or the side of the building. He reached down and picked up a large rock, readying himself to smash my face in.

Suddenly there was a screech of tires. A vintage T-bird rounded the corner followed by a powder blue Continental. They slammed to a halt in front of us, three men jumping out of the cars with machine guns.

"*Cuba libre, regresamos!*" one of them shouted. "Where are the tapes?"

Godzilla wheeled on them, pulling his .38 and firing instantly. He wasn't a bad shot at point-blank range. He hit the first two in the head, tearing their faces off and sending them flying back into the Continental in a spray of blood and gore. The third was hit in the chest, mortally wounded. He weaved along the sidewalk in a dance of death, stumbling forward and back, until he lurched sideways, grabbed onto a lamppost and spun around. His body was wrenching and shaking like a bull with its aorta cut. I thought he was going to collapse when, with a last Herculean effort, he raised his machine gun and fired, splattering Godzilla's guts all over the door of the House of Dominance. Then he, too, slumped to the ground. I walked over to him, the last dead Cuban. It was Santiago Martin. He had answered my phone call.

I took a deep breath and leaned against the lamppost, staring down at the mess around me. It was a sea of misdirected protoplasm; a lot of mothers and fathers who did a rotten job. Then I looked over at the House of Dominance, bleakly contemplating the blood-spattered door. I was trying to decide whether to go in when the police drove up.

"All right, who called?" It was Koontz. "Oh, it's you. Chairman Mao's favorite private eye."

"Chairman Mao doesn't like private eyes, Koontz. They're petit bourgeois individualists."

"Propaganda," he snapped. "Who are these creeps?"

"They shot each other."

"That's obvious. I asked who they were."

"These three are some Cubans who ran an outfit known as the Sexual Liberation League. This one over here, the blond monster, works for the Attorney General."

"What!"

"I said he works for the Attorney General."

"What kind of bullshit are you throwing around, peeper? You want me to slap you in the can?"

"No. But you can slap me in the face if you want."

Koontz didn't get it.

"All right," he said. "Enough of your paranoid accusations. Now tell me how you fit into all this?"

"I was just, uh, passing through."

"Passing through? Someone phoned my office half an hour ago saying he had something so sensational . . ."

"It could be."

"Could be? It better be!"

I nodded toward the House of Dominance. "How about us doing a little breaking and entering, Koontz, just between friends?"

"Now, wait a minute . . ."

"Come on now. It was good enough for the President, wasn't it? It's good enough for us."

He gave me a dirty look, but he didn't say anything when I lifted my leg and kicked in the door of the House. He followed me inside.

"What're we supposed to be looking for?"

"Dolores."

"Dolores?"

"See Dolores — she delivers!"

"But there's nobody here."

He was right about that. The place was empty, cleaned out, either hit by Dichter's campaign or out of luck on its own. There wasn't even much evidence of the kind of racket they had been running. No whips. No spikes. No leather. The booths had been dismantled. The closets were bare.

We proceeded on to the back room, a kind of service porch with a broken-down washing machine, sink and hot water heater. The room was musty, decayed. I was beginning to think I had deduced it all wrong when Koontz pointed at the floor.

"You idiot! There's your Dolores!" I followed his finger into the corner where a small, plastic kitty dish was stationed by the back door, the name "Dolores" written beneath the portrait of a smiling kitty. "You really fucked up this time, Wineberg!"

"Did I?" I said, stooping down to the dish. With a wink at Koontz I picked it up, revealing three black Memorex tape cassettes. I had to admit Hecht had a sense of humor, even before he shot himself.

23

"Can we go ahead, Señor Dichter?"

"Go ahead?"

"Yes, you know, with the massage stores in Playa del Rey."

"I believe so."

"But did you take care of the police?"

"What?"

"Did you take care of the police the way you did in Newport and Corona del Mar?"

"Yes, of course . . . Don't you trust me?"

"Trust you, señor? We'll always trust you."

"Good."

"Because we are recording this phone call, señor!"

"You're what!"

I sat there at the police station with Koontz as he played the tapes. Dichter's conversations made John Ehrlichman seem like St. Francis of Assisi. With any luck he would get a heavy reprimand for this and lose his license to practice law in San Bernardino.

While we were on the last cassette, I made a quick call to Alberts at the Sacramento *Bee* and gave him the scoop I had promised, just in case Koontz or some "secretary" accidentally erased the evidence.

Then I went home. The house was dark and the babysitter was asleep in front of the television, Johnny Carson blabbing away with the author of a new book on how to seduce your neurotic plants. The guy had the cover propped up in front of the camera and was selling books like crazy. This glimpse of the publishing industry sent my mind reeling back to Jock and Deborah — and to Nancy, standing there watching them, learning her lesson in sexual liberation. I had to sit down in a corner of the living room and press my hands to my temples, forcing myself to confront what had happened. Was Nancy's response crazy or a near-normal reaction to what was going on in front of her? In Italy, a man would be completely exonerated for such a "crime of passion," maybe never even brought to trial. But Nancy was a woman in a society that denied women the emotional excesses of men and the accompanying public privileges. And what about Jock? His behavior was disgusting, but it was hard to hate him. He had hated himself enough already, felt enough guilt to take his own life while having the foresight to expose public corruption by sending me a clue.

Sexual liberation was a tough bastard. I knew that from my own experience, my own jealousy and possessiveness. I remembered how, when we were first married, I couldn't stand Suzanne's descriptions of other guys she had slept with and how, later, I was unable to allow Alora the freedom I took for myself. I could always sense my own fear, even terror, of challenging those sexual preconceptions that had been welded to me since childhood, even harder to alter than the deepest needs for power and material possessions.

Unable to sleep, I stayed up all night trying to figure out what to do about Nancy. There was no hope in hiding it. Koontz was hot on the case and even he would be able to discover what had happened in a relatively short time. And then, with Reagan in Sacramento beating the drum for capital vengeance . . .

By the small hours of the morning I had narrowed it down to two choices. One, we could flee the country together, just get our passports and go, fly to South America before Koontz was able to sit down with the police commissioner and chart a course through this delicate case. The complications of such a move were staggering. What would we do about our children, our lives? How could we arrange it all in the few hours available?

Or two, I could turn her in. Leave it all at the mercy of the courts. The prospect was anything but pleasing. Then I thought of Diana Fields, an old law school friend of mine who was now practicing in L.A. 'She had a brilliant reputation as a trial lawyer, and if anyone knew how juries would dispose of this, she would. I dialed Diana and woke her up at four in the morning. After a moment of profuse apology and explanation, she listened to my story. She had some ideas all right. She said if we could picture Hecht as the worst shmuck of the last decade, and if Nancy turned herself in before the police apprehended her, we might be able to get her off with temporary insanity or involuntary manslaughter. Diana thought Nancy could be a free woman in four to six years.

I was ecstatic. I asked Diana if she would take the case, but she was very busy, backed up with several rapes and a landmark situation in child molestation. But I begged and she agreed.

I took a quick shower and paced around the living room, waiting for dawn. As soon as it came, I woke the babysitter and asked her to stay a while longer, telling her I would be back later in the day. Then I sped over to the Marmont, arriving at Nancy's bungalow before the clock had reached seven.

I knocked on the door and she opened it pretty quickly. From the rings around her eyes, it was clear she hadn't slept the previous night either. We embraced briefly and I went into the kitchenette to make some coffee. We sat down over a couple of cups in the living room as I explained to her what Diana had told me on the telephone three hours before. If Nancy turned herself in, Diana might be able to move quickly, to be at the police station and sign the proper statements before Koontz got the jump on us.

Nancy agreed. I finished my coffee while she went into the bathroom, washed and dressed. When she came out, wearing a plain black dress and no make-up, she looked about ten years younger, pale and redheaded like an eighteen-year-old Irish girl on her way to take her vows at the convent. I stood and met her at the door, wondering how we would feel about each other four or five years later when she got out of prison.

"You look good," I said.

"Thanks."

"You feeling all right?"

"Better."

"So am I."

We opened the door and went outside. It was a sunny morning and the patio of the Chateau Marmont was bathed with clear, southern California light. We walked away from the bungalow, down the sidewalk past some azalea bushes and the swimming pool. Then we turned, crossing to the right where I had parked the rented Vega at the side of Marmont Lane. I paused for a moment, stretching, trying to shake off the lethargy of a sleepless night. Nancy walked a few feet ahead and stopped, smiling back at me.

"Beautiful day," she said.

I nodded and moved to catch up with her.

It was then that I heard it — a dull, slapping noise like the sound of a medicine ball landing on a gymnasium canvas. But distant, remote. Nancy twisted, balanced on her left leg as if in a pirouette, and uttered a strained, inaudible cry, suddenly pitching backward in the direction of the swimming pool. A fountain of blood sprayed out of the front of her neck.

I screamed and ran forward, picking her up in my arms, searching frantically for her assailant among the trees and houses above me. But no one was to be seen in the dense, green landscape. The shot could have come from anywhere.

It was a very professional execution.

I turned away and clutched Nancy to me, her lifeless head swiveling against my shoulder, a wild turkey shot dead at four hundred yards.

24

This time Greenglass consented to see me. He was seated in a wheelchair in the library, looking even greener than before, a copy of *Barron's* business weekly across his lap.

"So you were using me as a pawn the whole time?"

"Let's say we were helping each other."

"Helping?"

"I needed someone outside the prison to test out my theories. Somebody smart. A nice Jewish boy like you."

"Thanks a lot, Greenglass."

"A nice *boychik* like you," he repeated, disregarding my sarcasm.

"Or Jock Hecht?"

"Jock was a nice *boychik* too. A little wild perhaps. But nice. Nicer than he thought . . . It's too bad they couldn't get together."

"He and Debbie?"

Meyer nodded, starting to cough and covering his mouth with the sleeve of his prison gown.

"You introduced them, didn't you?"

"Yeah."

"Why'd you do that?"

"I knew the kind of girl she was. She needed somebody

big, somebody important like a congressman or a senator or a famous writer. Otherwise she wouldn't have done anything. She wouldn't have wanted to get married."

"You cared that much whether she got married?"

He started to answer but his coughing resumed, this time more violently. He clutched his blanket around him and forced himself to stop. It was obvious he was a man of iron will. "Excuse me," he said. "What were you saying?"

"Never mind . . . Just tell me this. How did you know Meiko was in that air-conditioning duct?"

"You think I had her killed?"

"No. I just want to know."

He smiled. "For the record?"

"For the record."

"Well, I wasn't so sure who killed Deborah. It could have been the *shikse*; it could have been somebody else. I knew it wasn't Jock; he wouldn't have done it. So when he left that note, I knew he was either covering for his wife or it was a phony. I also knew that if it was a phony, they would have to get Meiko. And since I knew Meiko was in that movie and since I read the motion picture trade papers and since I know something from the old days about getting rid of bodies . . ."

"You figured it was Meiko who was freezing production." Greenglass nodded.

"But the note was genuine. At least he really wrote it and really committed suicide . . . so who killed Meiko?"

"Who do you think?"

I stopped for a moment. "I don't know. Someone forced into it."

"Why?"

"She was tortured, probably right there on the stage. And then they had to get rid of her quickly, after they got what they wanted and before she could rat on them."

"And what did they want?"

"What everybody wanted. The tapes. And she knew where they were, at least for a while."

"How did she know?" His question was sharp, acerbic. I

168

felt like I was being catechized by a gangster Socrates.

"She knew the operation, the League. She worked at the Phrontistery. And she knew Hecht. My guess is that she gave him the tapes, sold them to him probably, and then was tortured and killed for her trouble."

"Why do you guess that?"

"It makes sense. The only person in the world who knew Hecht had the tapes at that time was the person who gave them to him. She's tortured and then his files are broken into in a matter of hours."

"Good, *boychik*. So who kills her?"

"Santiago, who else? And that explains why Rhonda got so antsy when I mentioned Meiko on my first visit to the Phrontistery."

"Very smart." He folded up his magazine and looked at me. "But you shouldn't be a detective. You shouldn't waste your time on that. It counts for nothing in this world. You should be a doctor or a lawyer. Get into politics or business. Do something with yourself . . . And stay away from *goyim*. There are only two kinds of people in the world, listen to me, I know: Jews and anti-semites."

"When I want your advice, Greenglass, I'll ask for it!" I shouted at him.

"Getting angry?"

"Why'd you kill her, Greenglass?"

"Kill who? The *shikse?*"

"Yeah, the *shikse!*"

"What do you think? I should let her go in the courts? You were in love with her the first time you came in here. I could see that right away. You'd have gotten her out in six months to play with her baby girl. And when I heard you'd checked her back into the Marmont . . ."

"Oh, come on!"

"Don't you know Mosaic Law. An eye for an eye! A tooth for a tooth!"

"Who do you think you are? Jehovah?"

He slowed down and shook his head. "Moses . . . Moses

169

. . . Let me tell you a story."

"I don't want to hear any more of your stories, Meyer!"

"This one you want to hear."

"No. I don't."

"Yes, you do. Listen . . . listen . . ." He raised his feeble hand into the air. I felt like swinging at him, but I restrained myself. "Back in Vegas, '47, '48, around then, there was a singer, Rosie Green, from Philadelphia. I was running the Palm Casino at the time . . . and the Silver Fox. She sang at the Silver Fox with a band called the Injunaires. We had an affair. Those were stupid days, remember, nobody knew about contraceptives. Rubbers break, you know how it is . . . Rosie got pregnant. She wanted to go down to Mexico, have an abortion. I was going to send her, but something happened to me. I had never had a kid before. You know how it is, a gangster . . . You don't want to do it to children . . . Anyway, I paid her five thousand dollars to have the baby in England. When she came back, I took the baby from her and gave her to my brother-in-law Maxie in the movie business, so he could raise her good and proper. Bring her up in Beverly Hills. Get her a good education. A career. Marriage . . . So now you guess. That was Debbie Frank. The *shikse* killed my little girl, my only child . . . And let me tell you something else, if it makes you any happier. This yellow skin of mine, this cough — I have cancer of the pancreas. The doctors say I'm going to die in five, six months. So that's another reason she was killed. I didn't have time to wait to see what happened."

Greenglass began to cough again, this time more softly, his eyes watering. I turned and walked out of the library.

170

25

The following Saturday I went to retrieve my car. I had put it off longer than I should have, but I hadn't felt like visiting Topanga. I had been depressed, and it would have reminded me too much of Nancy and the case and I hadn't been ready to face that.

But it was a hot day, in the low eighties, and we had nothing to do; so the kids and I took the bus out to Santa Monica and hitched a ride up the Coast Highway in a VW convertible. We were dropped at the mouth of Topanga, where the hippies sell leather bracelets and imitation Persian rugs, and I cadged us another ride up to the shopping center in an orange Dodge piled high with surfboards. The driver was a tow-headed kid about seventeen whose hair was damp and who was still wearing the bottom half of his wetsuit. He didn't seem like he was in much of a hurry, so I convinced him to go a little out of his way and turn up Fernwood to the Institute.

In a short while we had reached the Jag. It appeared to be in good shape considering what happened, but I slipped inside and turned the engine over before waving good-bye to the surfer. He took off again with a wave and a couple of quick beeps on the horn of his van. I went outside again, unlocking the trunk and handing the jack to Jacob, while I wiggled out the spare tire and placed it alongside the second spare I had brought from town. Then I leaned down and wedged rocks under the front tires. The original spare looked pretty bald, but it would probably get us to the garage. I went around back again and started jacking up the car, all the while trying not to think about Nancy or that last moment at the Marmont when she turned with a smile, as if to tell me what a beautiful day it was, just before that muffled snap from the hills behind us.

I tried, but I couldn't. The image of her falling backward, her neck spouting red, kept coming back, like it had all week at any hour of the day or night.

I stopped pumping the handle and stared blankly into the back seat of the car.

"You're in a bad mood, Dad?" said Jacob.

"Yeah, I'm in a bad mood."

"What's the matter?"

"Sometimes things work out and sometimes they don't," I said, and resumed pumping. Jacob studied me, dissatisfied with my reply. Jacob knew me pretty well, but I didn't feel like explaining the situation, not right now anyway. I pushed harder on the jack. When the rear end of the car was halfway up, Jacob tugged on my sleeve again.

"Look," he said.

I paused and followed his gaze, but I couldn't see anything.

"What is it?"

"Skinny-dippers."

"Skinny-dippers?"

He pointed in the direction of a grove of live oaks at the top of the ridge. Sure enough, there were about a dozen naked people coming down the side. When they drew closer, I could see they all wore flowers around their necks and were holding hands, dancing along to a woman playing madrigals on the recorder. Among them I recognized Cindy, Gruskow, Lars Gundersen, Gunther, Anthony and several familiar faces from the Institute. We watched them descend until Gruskow noticed me.

"It's Moses Wine — the private dick!" he shouted, leading

them toward us at a run. "Hurray for Moses Wine. We heard about you — solving the Hecht case and putting the sonofabitch Dichter behind bars."

"Quite brilliant," said Lars Gundersen. "Your orchestration of the deaths of the thugs reminds me of Ray's *They Drive By Night* and the early Howard Hawks."

"Funny. I thought they were real people."

"You have inspired me, Mr. Wine."

"Lars has decided on the premise of his gangster movie," said Gruskow. "Corruption in the pornography business. A big-time politician in control of sex parlors murders a starving Chicano who is trying to expose him."

"It is a symbol of your society at this moment in history," the Swedish director explained. "From top to bottom it is, shall we say, pornographic."

"We had to bump Zimmerman," Gruskow added confidentially. "He couldn't cut it. But we have just the writer to do it for us now . . . None other than the great Dr. Gunther Thomas himself!"

"They have me on exclusive, man," Gunther apologized. "We'll have to wait on the *Rolling Stone* number." The woman playing the recorder launched into another madrigal. "You don't mind, do you?"

I shook my head and the others began dancing again, clapping hands and making a circle around us just like a Fellini flick. Simon watched them for a moment, then began to clap his hands too, joining in. But Jacob and I just stood there.

"Come on," said Cindy. "What're you so depressed about?"

"It's Nancy Hecht," said Gunther. "That's what's bothering him!"

"Ah, the hell with it!" echoed one of the others. "You can't go on being depressed forever!"

The music picked up and with it the tempo of their dancing. They circled around me faster and faster, chanting, "Come on! Come on! Come on!" Anthony separated from the group and passed me a jug of wine. "Don't be a jerk, mate. She's

173

been dead for a week. Let this be her Polish funeral."

I swilled from the bottle. "Huzzah!" said Cindy. The others applauded. "Now dance!" she said, taking Jacob and me and pulling us to the others, breaking open a spot in the ring.

"Dance, man! Dance!" they shouted. And I danced, reluctantly at first, but then faster, my feet racing out from under me, the sun beating down on my shoulders. I poured another swig of wine down my throat and laughed, throwing my head back. I hugged the people next to me, kissing them, and then I picked my kids up, swirling them around in the air. Beads of perspiration rolled down my back and forehead. The sun was becoming hotter and hotter. Soon, I was taking off my clothes.